The author of more than fifty books, with over 15 million copies in print, Arthur C. Clarke is one of the most distinguished figures in modern science and science fiction. He is the inventor of the concept of the communications satellite, a past Chairman of the British Interplanetary Society and a member of the Academy of Astronomics.

In 1969, he shared an Oscar nomination with Stanley Kubrick for *2001: A Space Odyssey,* the ground-breaking science fiction film. He has also covered the missions of Apollo 11, 12 and 15 with Walter Cronkite and NASA's Wally Schirra. In 1968 Mr. Clarke was selected to write the epilogue to the astronauts' own account of the Apollo mission, *First on the Moon.*

THE ROAD TO SPACE
The Earth from a height of 57 miles

ARTHUR C. CLARKE

AN INTRODUCTION TO ASTRONAUTICS

INTERPLANETARY FLIGHT

BERKLEY BOOKS, NEW YORK

Berkley books by Arthur C. Clarke

AGAINST THE FALL OF NIGHT
DOLPHIN ISLAND
INTERPLANETARY FLIGHT
THE PROMISE OF SPACE
THE SENTINEL

This Berkley book contains the complete
text of the original hardcover edition.
It has been completely reset in a typeface
designed for easy reading, and was printed
from new film.

INTERPLANETARY FLIGHT

A Berkley Book/published by arrangement with
Harper & Row, Publishers

PRINTING HISTORY
Harper & Row edition published 1950
Berkley edition/February 1985

ISBN: 0-425-06448-4

A BERKLEY BOOK ® TM 757,375
Berkley Books are published by The Berkley Publishing Group,
200 Madison Avenue, New York, New York 10016.
The name "BERKLEY" and the stylized "B" with design are
trademarks belonging to Berkley Publishing Corporation.
PRINTED IN THE UNITED STATES OF AMERICA

To David

CONTENTS

LIST OF PLATES

NOTE ON 1985 PRINTING

Interplanetary Flight was the first book of mine ever to be printed, and I therefore regard it with particular affection. I am delighted that it is now being reissued, 35 years after it was first published.

As the book's genesis has recently been described in Chapters 15–18 of *Ascent to Orbit: A Scientific Autobiography* (John Wiley), I will give only the basic facts here. While taking my degree at King's College, London, after leaving the Royal Air Force in 1946, I managed to find enough spare time to do a surprising amount of freelance writing. This included a two-part article, "Principles of Rocket Flight," for the leading British aviation journal, *The Aeroplane* (January 3 and 10, 1947). The article attracted the attention of Jim Reynolds, a senior editor at Temple Press, who was then planning a series of booklets under the general title "Technical Trends." Some of the other subjects in this series were *Mechanized Agriculture, Modern Railway Motive Power* and *The Industrial Gas Turbine*. To have included interplanetary travel under the same umbrella (in 1949!) was daring indeed, and I have often wondered what fights Jim Reynolds had with his directors before he sent me the contract.

The book was written between July and September 1949, when I was moonlighting from my job as an assistant editor at the Institution of Electrical Engineers. The first British edition appeared on May 1, 1950, and I dedicated it to a young college classmate named David Fowke (now Commander, Royal Navy–*retired*, which gives me quite a jolt). I also note, with some interest, that it was not until a week after publication that I received the advance: fifty pounds.

Interplanetary Flight was one of the very first books in the English language to give the basic theory of space travel in any technical detail, and a surprising number of people (including Dr. Carl Sagan and some of the astronauts) have told me how it aroused their interest in the subject, by revealing to them that space travel was more than fiction. It changed their lives, they said: it certainly changed mine, because its unexpected popularity caused Jim Reynolds to suggest that I write a second, non-technical, book for the general public. *The Exploration of Space* became a Book-of-the-Month Club selection in 1952, and propelled me into full-time authorship.

This sequence of events was largely triggered by my editor at Harpers, George Jones, who discovered *Interplanetary Flight* on a visit to England, and brought out the U.S. edition in 1951. (It was actually printed in the UK, and is identical with the British edition except for the title and copyright page.) George had a particular interest in rockets; as an Air Force colonel, he had helped to plan the famous raid on Peenemünde, home of the V2. In 1953, when I mentioned that I was visiting Dr. Wernher von Braun in Huntsville, Alabama, he said, "Tell Wernher that I once did my best to kill him". On receiving this information, Dr. von Braun laughed, reached into his desk, and pulled out a collection of 'morning after' photos of the bomb damage. "Tell George that he did a pretty good job", he said wryly.

Ten years later, in 1960, the book was revised by Dr. J. G. Strong, as I was then living in Ceylon (now Sri Lanka) and was much too busy exploring the shallower portions of the Indian Ocean (see *The Treasure of the Great Reef*, 1964) to concern myself with astronautics. Thereafter it was allowed to go out of print, as the momentum of events rapidly turned its forecasts into reality.

This reprinting of the original 1950 edition may serve as a vivid reminder of the truly incredible advances of the last four decades. Never in my wildest dreams could I have imagined, when I was writing the book in July 1949, that exactly twenty years later I would be standing at Cape Kennedy, since re-named Canaveral, watching the first men leave for the Moon.

The chapters on the Moon and planets also provide striking proof of the astronomical advances brought about by the Space Age. Looking back across the decades, it now seems that our knowledge of the Solar System was on a par with that of the medieval map-makers who filled their blanks with legends such as "Here be dragons." Alas, as far as our neighboring worlds are concerned, "Here be *no* dragons" now seems more appropriate.

My pleasure at seeing this book once more in print is tinged with sadness at the loss of so many of the friends—almost all of them fellow members of the British Interplanetary Society—who helped to make it possible. I am thinking particularly of Ralph Smith, Harry Ross, and especially of Val Cleaver, later Chief Engineer of the Rolls-Royce Rocket Division. And George Jones, who remained my editor at Harpers for almost twenty years, would have been especially delighted to know that 'his' book now has another lease on life; I grieve that the news came one month too late to tell him.

Arthur C. Clarke
Colombo, September 25, 1984

PREFACE

THIS BOOK is intended as a survey of the possibilities and problems of interplanetary flight, as far as they can be foreseen at the present day. Although the science of "astronautics" still belongs to the future, many of its basic conceptions will remain unaltered by the passage of time, and most of the fundamental techniques already exist in embryo. It is, for example, possible to calculate by quite simple methods the velocities and durations required for interplanetary journeys, irrespective of the physical means that may be used to accomplish them.

The attempt has been made throughout this book to keep the treatment quantitative, and to give exact values and magnitudes rather than vague generalities. Nevertheless, almost all mathematics has been relegated to the appendix, and it is believed that the argument can be followed without undue difficulty even by readers with little mathematical or scientific training. For those who wish to obtain a rapid overall view of the subject, without going into technicalities, it is suggested that Chapters I, VIII, IX and X be read first.

The approach throughout has been from the astronomical rather than the engineering point of view. The author makes no apologies for this, as there are now several excellent books on rocket technology, but none, at least in English, which develop the theory of astronautics in any detail.

It is a great pleasure to acknowledge the unfailing assistance of the officers of the British Interplanetary Society during the preparation of this book: they must not, however, be considered necessarily responsible for the views herein expressed. My particular gratitude is due to Mr. A. V. Cleaver for his critical reading of the manuscript and his continuous, and occasionally successful, attempts to make me appreciate the feelings of an engineer when confronted with some of the problems of space-flight—such as, for example, the handling of a thousand tons of liquid hydrogen.

Thanks are also due to the following for the loan of illustrations: G. Edward Pendray, for Plate II (from his "Coming Age of Rocket Power"); H. E. Ross for Plates X and XI; K. W. Gatland for Plates IV and VIII; R. A. Smith for Plates XIV and XV; and "Air Trails" and Frank Tinsley for Plate XIII.

Chapter I.

HISTORICAL SURVEY

THE DREAM of interplanetary travel is as old as the dream of flight: indeed, for many centuries both were inextricably entangled. If one could fly at all, men believed, then presumably it would be possible to go to the Moon, or even to the Sun. So it was thought in the days before Galileo and Newton, when the old mediæval ideas of the universe still held sway. The Moon might be fairly distant, it was true; but it could hardly be more remote than the fabulous lands of Hindustan or Cathay. The true immensity of astronomical space was still unrealized, and men were ignorant also of the fact that the atmosphere itself, which must support all the flying machines they could imagine, extended only a little way from the surface of the Earth. The slow understanding of these facts created a rift between aeronautics and "astronautics" that has lasted more than two hundred years, and is only now beginning to close. In the seventeenth century, reputable men of science could and did speculate freely about the possibility of voyages to the Moon, but thereafter the new knowledge damped earlier enthusiasms, and interplanetary flight became no more than a medium for fantasy and satirical fiction.

It remained thus during the years which saw the coming of the balloon, the first serious studies of heavier-than-air machines, and the final achievement of flight at the dawn of the twentieth century. With the conquest of the air assured, a few scientists of imagination turned once again

I

to the ancient dream, to see if the rising tide of technology had brought it any closer to realization.

The problem could now be stated in exact, quantitative terms and compared with the achievements of contemporary science. This was done almost simultaneously by Robert H. Goddard in the United States and Hermann Oberth in Roumania, both working independently but not unknown to each other. They are generally regarded as the founders of modern rocketry and astronautics, though priority for applying the rocket to the problem of space flight must go to the Russian, K. E. Ziolkovsky (1857-1936). The well-known French aeronautical engineer, Robert Esnault-Pelterie, had also made a study of the subject even before the First World War.

Goddard's aims were less ambitious than Oberth's, as is well shown by the titles of their first works—which were, respectively, *A Method of Reaching Extreme Altitudes* (1919) and *The Rocket into Planetary Space* (1923). The carefully non-sensational title of Goddard's paper was undoubtedly wise: even in 1945 he still felt compelled to write: "the subject of projection from the Earth, and especially a mention of the moon, must still be avoided in dignified scientific and engineering circles, even though projection over long distances on the earth's surface no longer calls for quite so high an elevation of eyebrows". Between 1915 and 1936, in a series of classic experiments, Goddard investigated almost every aspect of rocket design, and in March, 1926, he fired the world's first liquid-fuelled rocket at Auburn, Massachusetts. ((See Plate II.)

The claim has been made by some of his countrymen that Goddard is the father of modern rocketry, and on reading his two slim papers one is astonished by the clarity of his vision and the results he was able to accomplish with most limited resources. Moreover, though his nominal aim was the development of rockets for very-high-altitude meteorological research, he was fully aware of the subject's remoter applications. Even in his first paper he gave calculations showing the size of rocket necessary to reach the Moon with enough flash-powder to be visible from the Earth. There is no record of his making any predictions about interplanetary flight, though some cryptic remarks in his first book suggest that he had a good deal more in mind than merely sending a few pounds of flash-powder to the Moon[1].

Oberth had no such inhibitions, and his most important work, published in 1929, had the uncompromising title "The Way to Space Travel" (*Wege zur Raumschiffahrt*). In this remarkable book Oberth not only gave a thorough mathematical discussion of interplanetary flight, but also considered in great detail all the technical problems involved in the design of manned "spaceships" capable of travelling to the Moon and planets. He also devoted some attention to the possibility of artificial satellites, a subject which has now been taken up at official levels in the United States. Even today, there are relatively few aspects of the entire science of astronautics which Oberth did not foresee and discuss more than twenty years ago.

Oberth was a mathematician, not an experimental scientist, and his conclusions, unlike Goddard's, were based almost entirely on theoretical reasoning. But his work,

---

[1] "There are, however, *developments of the general method under discussion which involve a number of important features not herein mentioned*, which could lead to results of much scientific interest. These developments involve many experimental difficulties, to be sure; but they depend upon nothing that is really impossible." (Goddard's italics.)

because of its more dramatic content, had a much greater immediate influence than Goddard's patient but unspectacular investigations. A direct result of Oberth's writings was the formation in Germany of the "Society for Spaceship Travel" (*Verein für Raumschiffahrt*) which in the years 1929-1933 designed and fired many small liquid-fuelled rockets—and, thereby, trained not a few of the men who were later to make rocket development Germany's leading technical contribution to the War. The story of Peenemunde is one which has been told elsewhere [2] and need not be repeated here, but it is not always realised that German interest in rockets was originally stimulated by their interplanetary, and not their military, implications.

In the closing months of the War the astonishing results of a decade's intensive and secret research were revealed to the world. Achievements which rocket enthusiasts in other countries had suggested as possibilities of the future—with diffidence and in the face of ridicule or even hostility [3] —were suddenly found to belong already to the past. The result was, to some extent, the replacement of an ill-informed scepticism by an equally ill-informed enthusiasm. Many laymen, confronted by the gigantic technical achievement of the V.2. rocket and unaware of the years of patient development work behind it, imagined that it would not be long before world-wide or even interplanetary flights became possible. Reputable journals in the United States began discussing, in all seriousness, the military advantages

[2] See Willy Ley: *Rockets and Space Travel.*

[3] A reviewer in *Nature* wrote, on the appearance of P. E. Cleator's *Rockets Through Space* in 1936: "Mr. Cleator thinks it a pity that the Air Ministry evinced not the slightest interest in his ideas; provided that an equal indifference is shown by other Ministries elsewhere, we all ought to be profoundly thankful."

of Mars or the Moon as matters of fairly immediate importance.

These optimistic forecasts were largely stimulated by quite another technical advance—the release of atomic energy. Here was the fuel to conquer space: the engine already existed, and combining the two was only a matter of time—perhaps not very much time at that.

The truth, as usual, lies between the extremes. Among those competent to judge the matter, there are now very few who would not agree that the rocket provides the means for the exploration of space. (There are still a few pessimists even among the experts: but one must remember that Lord Rutherford never believed that atomic energy would be liberated, and Hertz pooh-poohed the idea that electromagnetic waves could ever be used for communication!) The chief conflict of opinion among the authorities concerns points of detail, and, in particular, the length of time likely to elapse before space flight becomes a reality. Some believe it may be little more than a decade in the future, while others put it a hundred years ahead. There is little doubt that many, if not all, of the fundamental problems of astronautics will be solved during the next fifty years, and it is quite possible that the same century which opened with the conquest of the air may also see the first exploration of the nearer planets.

The position of astronautics today is not unlike that of heavier-than-air flying in the closing years of the nineteenth century, when all the necessary fundamental knowledge was available and it remained only to apply it. But the parallel must not be taken too far. The first aeroplanes were made by individual experimenters at their own expense: the first spaceships will tax the resources of nations, for the problem is several orders of magnitude more difficult. Against this, however, must be set the fact that the efforts being devoted to rocket research are already incomparably greater than were those available to the science of aeronautics in its infancy. Out of this work, most of it now secret, will come the tools that can destroy our civilization or take it to the stars.

During the next few decades, the applications of the rocket will become steadily more numerous as it plays an ever-increasing part in the fields of civil and military aviation, of weapons development, and of fundamental scientific research. Yet these—the "terrestrial" applications —are merely a preparation and a prelude for its ultimate rôle, which will eventually overshadow all others. On the Earth, the rocket will be no more than yet another of many alternative forms of transport; but in space, it will be unique, taking men upon journeys which may shape the futures of more worlds than one—journeys which may bring again to mankind the breathless wonder of that golden Renaissance dawn, when the old horizons were receding, the ancient boundaries were being annihilated, and the foundations of new civilizations were being laid.

This is the dream : and now it remains to survey the long road that must be travelled before it can become reality.

Chapter II

THE EARTH'S GRAVITATIONAL FIELD

Escape Velocity

MAN IS still essentially a two-dimensional creature: all his journeys in the vertical direction have so far been of negligible extent. It is, therefore, perhaps not surprising that some very curious ideas persist about gravity—one of the commonest being that it ceases, more or less abruptly, at a definite distance from the Earth. The frequently-encountered phrase "beyond the Earth's gravity" is a good example of this survival from pre-Newtonian thinking.

Strictly speaking, no point in the Universe is "beyond the Earth's gravity", which decreases as the inverse square of the distance and so becomes zero only at infinity. At the greatest heights yet attained by rocket, its value is still nearly 90% of that at sea-level, and one must go to an altitude of 2620 kms (1630) miles before it is even halved.

Over astronomical distances, however, the decrease is extremely rapid, as an inspection of Figure 1 will show. The point beyond which, for practical purposes, the Earth's gravitational field may be neglected, depends entirely on the particular case being considered. As will be seen later, a body travelling at a very high speed quite close to the Earth will be far less affected by its field than a slow-moving body at a great distance. Thus the Earth is incapable of capturing a meteor skimming just outside the atmosphere at

7

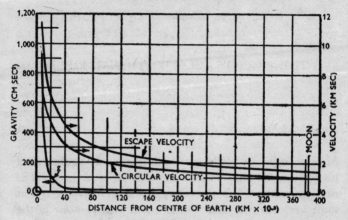

Fig. 1. Variation of gravity, and escape and circular velocities, with distance from Earth's centre.

50 km/sec, while it holds the Moon (moving at 1 km/sec) firmly chained in its orbit a thousand times further away.

Since the work done in lifting a body of unit mass vertically against the Earth's field is the product of distance times force, it follows that, for equal distances, this work decreases with height according to the inverse square law or the "g" curve of Figure 1. At ten radii from the Earth's centre, moving a body through a given vertical distance requires only a hundredth of the energy needed to perform the same feat at sea-level. The *total* energy, E, required to lift unit mass from the Earth's surface to "infinity" (or to a point where for all practical purposes gravity can be neglected) is clearly proportional to the area beneath the "g" curve in Figure 1. An integration (see Appendix) gives the surprisingly simple result:—

$$E = gR \qquad \dots \qquad \dots \qquad (\text{II.2})$$

where g is the value of gravity at the Earth's surface (981 cm/sec^2 or 32.2 ft/sec^2) and R is its radius (6360 kms or 3960 miles).

This equation makes possible a rather striking mental picture of the work involved in lifting or projecting a body completely away from the Earth. The energy expended in climbing a mile is something which can be visualized as not outside the range of normal experience, though only an Alpine guide would consider it part of the day's work. A jet fighter can climb ten miles vertically, and could repeat the performance several times before exhausting its fuel, while a V.2 rocket can ascend to a height of over a hundred miles. But as Equation II.2 shows, the escape from Earth is equivalent to a climb of one radius, or almost four thousand miles, under a gravity equal to its sea-level value.

This peculiarly simple law, which we will often invoke, holds for all planets and gravitating bodies. To take a case which, as will be seen later, is not as academic as it sounds, the escape from the Sun (whose radius and surface gravity are 109 and 28 times that of the Earth) is equivalent to a vertical climb of almost $109 \times 28 \times 4000$ miles, or approximately 12,000,000 miles (say 20,000,000 kms) against one terrestrial gravity. In the same way, the work required to leave any other body in the Solar System may be easily calculated.

Our position here on the Earth's surface may best be visualized by an analogy which will play an important part in later discussions. Since the escape from our planet is equivalent to a vertical ascent of four thousand miles against one gravity, we may picture ourselves as being at the bottom of a valley or crater four thousand miles deep, out of which we must climb if we are ever to leave the

Earth. The walls of this imaginary crater are at first very steep, but as Earth's gravity weakens they become slowly less vertical and the ascent correspondingly easier. At very great distances (a hundred thousand miles or more) the slope becomes more and more nearly horizontal until at last we have, for all practical purposes, reached the level plain and can move in any direction with no appreciable expenditure of energy.

This imaginary "gravitational pit" has been accurately drawn in Figure 2, which shows the amount of work

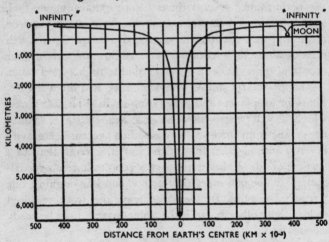

Fig. 2. Potential Energy Diagram of Earth-Moon System.

needed to reach "infinity" from any point within about 300,000 miles (500,000 kms) of the Earth. The figure must of course be regarded as three-dimensional, like the stem of an inverted wine-glass: its section is actually the rectangular hyperbola defined by Equation II.3.

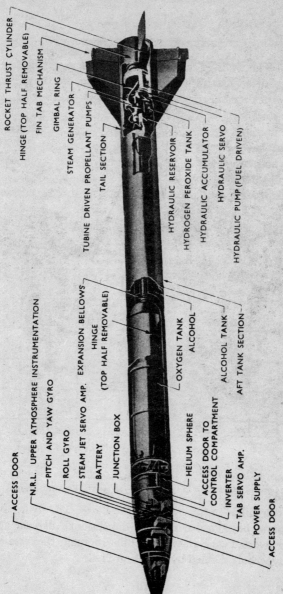

ROCKET THRUST CYLINDER
HINGE (TOP HALF REMOVABLE)
FIN TAB MECHANISM
GIMBAL RING
STEAM GENERATOR
TUBINE DRIVEN PROPELLANT PUMPS
TAIL SECTION
HYDRAULIC RESERVOIR
HYDROGEN PEROXIDE TANK
HYDRAULIC ACCUMULATOR
HYDRAULIC SERVO
HYDRAULIC PUMP (FUEL DRIVEN)

ACCESS DOOR
N.R.L. UPPER ATMOSPHERE INSTRUMENTATION
PITCH AND YAW GYRO
ROLL GYRO
STEAM JET SERVO AMP.
EXPANSION BELLOWS
HINGE (TOP HALF REMOVABLE)
BATTERY
JUNCTION BOX
HELIUM SPHERE
ACCESS DOOR TO CONTROL COMPARTMENT
INVERTER
TAB SERVO AMP.
POWER SUPPLY
ACCESS DOOR
OXYGEN TANK
ALCOHOL
ALCOHOL TANK
AFT TANK SECTION

VIKING RESEARCH ROCKET

Plate I

Plate II

Photograph: G. E. Pendray

A GENERATION OF ROCKET DESIGN I
Professor Goddard with the World's first Liquid-fuel rocket, Worcester, Mass.,
1926.

Plate III   *Photograph: Keystone.*

A GENERATION OF ROCKET DESIGN II
A V.2. being prepared for launching, White Sands, New Mexico, 1949.

Plate IV (above)   *By permission of the*
                    Ministry of Supply

"RHEINBOTE" STEP ROCKET

Plate V

THE FIRST LIQUID-FUEL-STEP-
ROCKET
(V.2 and "WAC Corporal")

Photograph: U.S. Army.

In the same way, all other celestial bodies have their exactly similar gravitational pits. That of the Sun, as we have already seen, is 12,000,000 miles or 20,000,000 kms deep. The Moon's, on the other hand, is only 170 miles (280 kms) deep, and is represented to scale by the small dimple far up the slope of the Earth's field in Figure 2. If we imagine this diagram as showing the profiles of two adjacent valleys, it will be seen that the problem of escape from the Moon is enormously simpler than that of leaving the Earth.

There are, in principle, two main ways in which a body can be transferred from the Earth's surface to infinity. It can be moved at a slow and more or less uniform speed, by the continuous application of some force; but this method, as will be seen later, is excessively wasteful of energy. Alternatively, it can receive the necessary kinetic energy in one instalment, as it were, by being given a velocity sufficient for it to "coast" up the slope of the gravitational crater under its own momentum before coming to rest. The velocity needed to do this is known as the escape or parabolic velocity: it is equal to $\sqrt{(2gR)}$ (Equation II.4) and its numerical value at the Earth's surface is 11.2 km/sec (7 miles/sec or 25,000 m.p.h.) This is also the velocity which a body would acquire during a fall to the Earth's surface from a very great distance: it follows therefore that a spaceship leaving the Earth must not only reach this speed on the outward journey but must also neutralize it on the return, if it is to make a safe landing.

Escape velocity, though usually quoted for the Earth's surface, naturally decreases with distance as a body starting at a considerable altitude would need less initial speed to reach infinity.[1] The rate of decrease is rather slow and is also shown in Figure 1. (the curve being given by Equation II.5).

This curve gives the same sort of information as Figure 2, but in a more useful and immediately understandable form. It shows at a glance the vertical projection velocity needed, at any point, to send a body right away from the Earth—and, conversely, the velocity a body initially at rest would acquire in falling to that point from a great distance.

A body projected from the Earth at less than escape velocity would of course fall back to the surface after reaching a certain height, and would, moveover, return to its initial point at exactly its original speed (if there were no air-resistance losses). It is instructive to consider the height a body would reach if projected outside the atmosphere at various speeds. Elementary text-books give the well-known equation:—

$$V^2 = 2gh$$

where V is the initial velocity and h the height attained. This equation, though accurate for distances of up to a few hundred miles, assumes that "g" is constant and so breaks down at great distances. (It states, in particular, that an infinite height is only reached at an infinite initial speed, which as we have seen is incorrect.)

The correct law is slightly more complicated (Equation II.7) and the results given by both are shown in Figure 3.

It will be seen that at the speeds reached by existing rockets, both laws serve equally well: but as projection speeds pass into the 4 kms/sec or 10,000 m.p.h. range and above,

---

[1] Anyone unduly disconcerted by the occasional appearance of the mathematical fiction "infinity" can substitute "a few million miles".

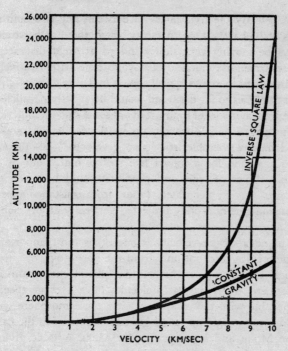

Fig. 3. Height-Projection Velocity Curve.

the heights attained increase rapidly, becoming infinite at the velocity of escape.

The remaining case of vertical projection which should be mentioned is that of a body leaving the Earth at a speed *greater* than escape velocity. In this case the body's speed, instead of falling gradually towards zero at a great distance, would fall towards some finite speed which it would always possess. The chief result of this excess velocity would be to reduce greatly the time of travel between any two points for a body barely able to escape from the Earth would always be moving very slowly indeed at great distances. The spectacular reduction of voyage time with relatively small velocity increases is well shown in Table 2 (page 56).

All the cases so far discussed would be exactly paralleled if one made a model of Figure 2 out of some smooth material and projected a ball-bearing up its slope. Such a model would have a characteristic "escape velocity" (about one metre a second for a model five metres high) and by a suitable choice of scale and profile it could be made to demonstrate very accurately (apart from resistance losses) the movements of a body projected vertically at any point or at any speed.

A planet's escape velocity is one of its most important characteristics, and not only from the view-point of astronautics. It determines whether that planet can retain an atmosphere, for if the gas molecules have average speeds comparable with the escape velocity, the atmosphere will quickly leak away into space—as has happened in the case of the Moon and is happening for Mars. A table giving this value for the more important bodies in the Solar System will be found in Chapter X.

Circular Velocity

Closely related to escape velocity is the conception of orbital or circular velocity, which is the speed at which a body would continue to circle the Earth indefinitely like a second Moon, its outward centrifugal force balancing the inward pull of gravity (just as one may whirl a stone at the end of a piece of string.) The necessary speed to maintain a stable orbit at any distance from the Earth is easily calculated (Equation II.8) and near the Earth's surface is about 7.9 km/sec (18,000 m.p.h.) This is less than the corresponding escape velocity in the ratio $1 : \sqrt{2}$, a proportion which holds universally at all points. It is, therefore, much easier for a body to become a close satellite of the Earth than to escape completely, a point which as we shall see later is of great importance. The conception of a rocket or other structure circling round the Earth forever with no expenditure of energy seems peculiarly difficult for the layman to understand—his usual reaction being: "Why doesn't it fall down?" Perhaps if, like Jupiter, our planet had a dozen or so natural satellites at varying distances, the idea of a few artificial ones would be more readily accepted.

Circular velocity, like escape velocity, decreases slowly with distance according to an inverse square *root* law, and the values of both for points out to the Moon's orbit are shown in Figure 1.

The time of revolution of a satellite in such orbits is of importance, and this may be readily calculated (Equation II.9). A body just outside the Earth's atmosphere would have a period of only $1\frac{1}{2}$ hours. If, like the Moon, it moved in the same direction as the Earth's spin, it would appear to rise in the *West* and set in the *East*, flashing across the sky in a few minutes[2]. An even more peculiar state of affairs would arise if the satellite's orbit had a radius of 42,000 kms (or a height of 22,000 miles) since then its period would be exactly 24 hours. It would thus revolve with the Earth,

[2] One case is actually known of a satellite with an orbital period shorter than its planet's day, and hence with such an apparent retrograde motion—Phobos, the inner moon of Mars.

and so would always appear fixed in the sky, being visible only from one hemisphere, over which it would never rise nor set. Some of the important implications of this will be examined in Chapter VIII (page 104) when the subject of "space-stations" is discussed.

Other Orbits

We have now considered the two simplest cases of movement possible for a body projected beyond the Earth's atmosphere at a point where the only force acting is that of gravity. It now remains to consider the more general case, where the motion is neither radial nor circular.

To fix ideas, imagine a point just beyond the atmosphere and consider what happens when a body is given various horizontal speeds. At 7.9 km/sec (5 miles/sec) it will, as we have seen, travel round the Earth forever in a circular orbit. A lesser speed will make it impossible to maintain this orbit and it will eventually fall to Earth—though it may travel half-way round the planet before doing so.

If the original speed is in *excess* of the orbital velocity, then the body will move outwards. It will recede from the Earth along an elliptical path, gradually losing speed until at the point farthest from the Earth ("apogee") its motion will again be tangential and it will be travelling at its lowest speed. Thereafter, unable to maintain itself at this distance, it will fall back with increasing velocity to its original point of projection ("perigee") and will continue to retrace its path indefinitely.

Given the initial distance from the Earth and the tangential velocity, it is a simple matter to calculate the major axis and eccentricity of the ellipse. (Equations II.10—14). The period can also be readily found: it is independent of the eccentricity and is the same as for the circular orbit whose diameter equals the major axis of the ellipse. Equation II.9 may thus be used to obtain the periods of elliptical as well as circular orbits.

As the initial velocity is increased, the ellipse becomes more and more elongated and the furthest point moves

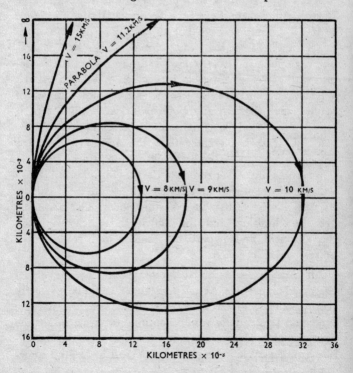

Fig. 4. Orbits in the Earth's Field.

steadily towards infinity. (Figure 4.) When escape velocity is reached, the ellipse changes into a parabola and the body never returns. (This is the reason why escape velocity is often called parabolic velocity.) For speeds greater than this value, the body moves away from Earth along a hyperbola, which at very great speeds indeed (over 100 km/sec) would become almost a straight line.

A few typical orbits, with perigee points just outside the Earth's atmosphere, have been accurately drawn in Figure 4. It will be appreciated that an infinity of possible orbits exists, ranging from the almost circular to the very elongated, with perigees at every possible distance from the Earth, and with corresponding velocities which may be calculated from Equation II.10. Moreover, an infinite number of orbits passes through any given point, and which type is chosen by a body at this point depends entirely on its velocity. If this is greater than the appropriate escape velocity at the point, the body will recede into space along a hyperbola and never return to Earth. If it is less, the body will remain captured in a closed orbit—unless, of course, its path intersects the Earth's atmosphere. The parabolic orbit is a limiting (and unstable) boundary case between the elliptical and hyperbolic families and could never be realized in practice.

All these cases could be demonstrated[3] by the model described on page 14. At any point there would be a velocity (corresponding to circular velocity) at which a particle projected tangentially would continue to circle inside the cone, keeping always the same distance from the apex—like a motor-cycle rider inside the "Wall of Death" some-

[3] Neglecting the effects of friction.

times seen at fun-fairs. If it was projected at too low a speed it would fall towards the centre, thus gaining speed, and after reaching its lowest point (and greatest velocity) would rise to the original point again, tracing a roughly elliptical orbit. In the same way, all the other elliptic and hyperbolic paths could be reproduced by varying the initial velocity of projection.

Summary

These various types of orbit have been discussed in some detail because they are of fundamental importance in any analysis of the problem of escape from Earth. Moreover, they apply not only to Earth but to all gravitating bodies; and, in particular, to the Sun. A body—be it planet, comet or spaceship—moving freely in the Sun's field must follow one or other of the paths we have been discussing. The problem of interplanetary flight is essentially one of choosing the most suitable orbit between two points, and then of achieving the initial speed necessary to travel along it. Thereafter no further expenditure of power is necessary until the time—which may be months or years later—when the gravitational field of the body of destination becomes dominant. In Chapter VI we shall see how to select the most economical, or the fastest, paths between two planets in the Solar System; and we shall also find, as in many terrestrial applications, that speed and economy are mutually exclusive.

The velocities needed to enter these orbits are very high by our present standards of speed. The simplest mission—that of projecting a body into a circular orbit around the Earth—requires a velocity of 18,000 m.p.h. To discuss the possibility of attaining such speeds, we must now consider the basic principles of rocket propulsion.

Chapter III

THE ROCKET

Fundamentals

THE ROCKET motor is unique among prime movers in two respects—its independence of any external medium, and its ability to generate colossal thrusts and powers. Both of these characteristics are required for space-flight, the former for obvious reasons, the second because very large masses of fuel are necessary for interplanetary missions.

No detailed discussion of the purely engineering aspects of the rocket will be given in this book, as several excellent works on the subject are now available. (See Bibliography). But it may be as well to spend some little time considering why the rocket, unlike all other forms of propulsion, can operate in space, which for all practical purposes is a perfect vacuum.

All forms of locomotion depend on reaction. Surface vehicles, through the friction of their wheels, try to thrust the Earth away from them and, to an immeasurably small extent, succeed; but such is the disparity of masses that the effect on the Earth is unnoticeable. Aeroplanes and ships operate by giving momentum to a mass of air or water, thus acquiring equal momentum in the reverse direction. This is most clearly seen in the case of the jet aircraft, the rocket's closest relative. The jet collects a large quantity of air, which it heats and expels at a very great velocity, thereby obtaining a thrust which is proportional to the product of the jet's mass and its increase in speed. If it could carry its own oxygen supply, instead of obtaining it from the air, a jet aircraft could then operate as a self-contained unit capable of functioning in a vacuum—and would, indeed, then be a type of rocket.

It cannot be too strongly emphasised that neither the rocket nor the jet obtains thrust by "pushing on the air behind", as a great many people believe. All the "push" occurs *inside* the combustion chambers and exhaust nozzles, and the subsequent adventures of the burnt gases once they have left the system can have no effect on it whatsoever. It is sometimes helpful to think of the rocket's still burning and expanding gases as thrusting against the already burnt gas further down the nozzle, so producing a recoil in exactly the same way as the charge in a gun, driving the bullet forwards, forces the gun backwards with equal momentum. The rocket may indeed be regarded as a sort of continuously operating gun firing out a stream of gas instead of solid material.

The velocity which a rocket can attain, after burning all its fuel, is clearly dependent on the speed with which the gases leave the nozzle (the exhaust or jet velocity) and the amount of fuel ejected. These quantities are connected by the simple relation (see Appendix), the most important in the whole of rocketry:—

$$V = c \log_e R \qquad \ldots \qquad \ldots \qquad (III.2)$$

where V is the rocket's final velocity, c is the jet velocity, and R is the "mass-ratio" or the ratio

$$\frac{\text{initial mass of rocket}}{\text{final mass of rocket after burning fuel}}$$

In common logarithms, this equation may be written

$$V = 2.3026 c \log_{10} R$$

Instead of R, it is sometimes more convenient (particularly in engineering discussions) to use the parameter ζ[1], defined as

$$\frac{\text{mass of fuel}}{\text{total mass of rocket}}$$

In this case Equation III.1 becomes:—

$$V = c \log_e \frac{1}{1-\zeta}$$

The inverse form of Equation III.1 is also very useful:—

$$R = e^{\frac{V}{c}} \quad \ldots \quad \ldots \quad \text{(III.2.a)}$$

where e is the transcendental number 2.71828....

From these equations, it follows that although the rocket's speed increases in direct proportion to exhaust speed, it does so only slowly with increase in mass-ratio. This result is best shown graphically, as in Figure 5.

These curves show that, for a given value of exhaust-velocity c, impossibly high values of mass-ratio R would be needed if the rocket is to attain a final speed much greater than c. For $R = e = 2.718...$, the rocket's final speed would equal its jet speed. This value presents no engineering difficulties: it would mean, for example, building a rocket of empty mass 1 ton, carrying 1.72 tons of fuel. V.2 did considerably better than this, having a mass-ratio of over 3 with its normal one ton warhead, and almost 4 if carrying only light meteorological instruments. But to *double* the final speed, with the same exhaust velocity, would mean *squaring* the mass-ratio, i.e. increasing it from 2.72 to 7.4

---

[1] Also called the mass-ratio by some writers. There is no possibility of confusion, however, as R is always greater than 1 and ζ is always less.

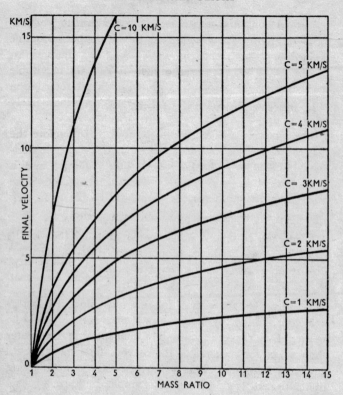

Fig. 5. Rocket Velocity as a function of Mass-Ratio and Jet Velocity.

(e^2). This would be a considerable technical feat, though perhaps not an impossible one. A rocket capable of travelling three times as fast as its exhaust would need a mass-ratio of 20 (e^3), which may be regarded as quite impracticable, since it would require that 95 % of the machine's total mass be fuel and only the remaining 5 % be devoted to payload, structure, motors, etc. It appears, therefore, that no simple rocket can be built to travel more than 2 or 3 times as fast as its exhaust. When, as in the next chapter, the inevitable losses due to air-resistance and gravitational retardation are considered, it will be seen that the value 2 is more likely to be the upper limit.

The attainment of high exhaust speeds is therefore the first concern of the rocket engineer, and is a problem involving chemistry, thermodynamics, metallurgy, and a great deal of still somewhat empirical mathematics. The *absolute maximum* of exhaust velocity available from any given fuel is easily calculated by assuming that the motor converts all the propellant's energy of combustion into kinetic energy at 100 % efficiency. The figure obtained in this way, however, has very little relation with reality. In practice, owing to the inevitable losses in any heat engine, no more than about 70 % of this theoretical or ideal velocity can ever be achieved: with current designs, the figure is about 55 %.

The best-known rocket fuel (that used in V.2) is the alcohol-liquid oxygen combination with an ideal exhaust velocity of about 4.2 km/sec (14,000 f.p.s.) The value realized so far in practice is only some 2.25 km/sec (7,500 f.p.s.)

Considerably more powerful fuels exist, with ideal exhaust velocities of up to 6.5 km/sec (21,000 f.p.s.). These involve "combustion", not with oxygen, but with the still more reactive element fluorine. When such propellants are fully developed (which will require many years of research and considerable improvements in metallurgy to permit motor operation at high temperatures) it is possible that exhaust speeds of around 4.5 km/sec (15,000 f.p.s.) may be obtained. It can be shown [2] that, *irrespective of the energy contained in any possible propellant*, this figure is near the absolute limit which may be achieved with chemical rockets, since much higher values would require impossible temperatures and pressures in the motor. The argument is on the following lines.

The rocket is a heat-engine which operates according to the well-known thermodynamic laws applying to all such engines. Given the conditions of temperature, pressure, gas composition, etc. inside the combustion chamber, it is possible to calculate the velocity with which the exhaust gases will emerge. It is found that the exhaust velocity c of the gases is largely determined by their molecular weight M and their initial temperature T before expansion. The complete equation is given in the appendix (Equation III.3) but for a rocket working in a vacuum and with a given propellant combination we have the simple approximate result:—

$$c \sim k\sqrt{T/M} \quad \dots \quad \dots \quad \text{(III.4)}$$

k being a constant.

In the chemical rockets so far employed the exhaust gases have been largely steam ($M=18$) and the carbon oxides ($M=28$ and 44). With a few rare exceptions which may not be of practical value, there are no highly-energetic chemical reactions giving end products with molecular weights much lower than these values. The main hope of

[2] See, for example, Cleaver, "Interplanetary Flight: Is the Rocket the only Answer?": *Journal of the B.I.S.*, 6, 127-48 (June 1947); or Seifert, Mills and Summerfield, "The Physics of Rockets": *American Journal of Physics*, 15, 121-40 (March-April, 1947).

Plate VI

SPACESHIP DESIGNED BY HERMANN OBERTH
(*from the film "Frau im Mond,"* 1929).

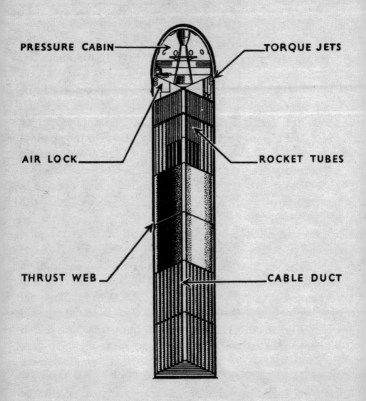

PRESSURE CABIN

TORQUE JETS

AIR LOCK

ROCKET TUBES

THRUST WEB

CABLE DUCT

Plate VII

"*CELLULAR*" *SPACESHIP: B.I.S.* 1939.

improved performance therefore lies in an increase of the operating temperature T, since we can do little about M.

Maximum present-day rocket combustion temperatures are of the order of 2,800°C (5,000°F). That motors can be built for continuous operation at temperatures so much above the melting point of their material (1300 °C or 2300°F for the mild steel used in V.2) is due to the employment of elaborate cooling systems. Making fairly optimistic assumptions about future progress in this direction, it appears that motors may eventually be built to operate at temperatures and pressures yielding exhaust velocities around 4—4.5 kms/sec.

It must be pointed out that the above argument is quite general and depends in no way upon the energy content of any particular fuel. There are in fact not many fuels which could liberate enough energy to provide this limiting performance. And if—as seems unlikely from fundamental chemical considerations—a "super-fuel" was discovered which gave much more energy, it could not be handled for these purely physical reasons. At the moment, in fact, we cannot use many of the best fuels which we do possess. Even the alcohol used in V.2 had to be "watered-down", with an appreciable loss of performance, to prevent the motor burning out.

A table giving some of the more important propellants known at present or likely to be used in the near future is given overleaf, together with their exhaust velocities in km/sec. These values can only be somewhat approximate as they would vary from motor to motor or in the same motor from sea-level to vacuum.

Since we have seen that it is not practicable to build a rocket capable of travelling more than about twice as fast

Table 1
ROCKET PROPELLANT EXHAUST VELOCITIES

Propellant	Exhaust velocity (km/sec.)
Oxygen and petrol	2.5
Oxygen and methane (CH_4)	2.6
Oxygen and ethanol (C_2H_5OH)	2.5
Oxygen and ammonia (NH_3)	2.6
Oxygen and hydrazine (N_2H_4)	2.8
Oxygen and hydrogen	3.6
Oxygen and diborane (B_2H_6)	3.2
Nitric acid and aniline ($C_6H_5NH_2$) ...	2.2
Nitric acid and petrol	2.4
Fluorine and hydrogen	3.8
Fluorine and hydrazine	3.2
Hydrogen peroxide (H_2O_2) and petrol ...	2.3
Hydrogen peroxide and C-stoff[3]	2.1
Hydrogen peroxide (as monopropellant) ...	1.2
Nitromethane (CH_3NO_2) (as monopropellant)	2.2

These values are calculated for reasonable motor losses and chamber pressures as used in existing rockets. Optimum mixture ratios and negligible back-pressure (*i.e.*, vacuum operation) have been assumed. Values about 10 per cent. higher would be obtained if chamber pressures were doubled.

as its exhaust, it would therefore seem that—even when chemical propellants and motors have been developed to the ultimate—we cannot hope to built rockets capable of attaining speeds of over 9 km/sec (20,000 m.p.h.) This would be sufficient to achieve circular velocity, but insufficient for an escape from the Earth. In later chapters, however, we

[3] A methanol-hydrazine-water mixture, used in the Me.163 rocket fighter.

will see that there are various ways of avoiding this difficulty, notably by the principle of "step construction".

Speeds of 20,000 m.p.h., however inadequate for interplanetary purposes, are of course enormous by any standards existing before the advent of the rocket. Even after allowing for the various losses discussed in the next chapter, they would enable rockets to rise to heights of the order of 6,000 kms (4,000 miles) and so would open up whole new fields of scientific research and investigation.

Since the high-altitude research rocket will be the precursor of the spaceships to be discussed later, it may be as well to end this chapter with a brief description of a typical modern design—the Martin-Reaction Motors' "Viking". This machine, though following the basic V.2 layout, incorporates a number of advances and is the highest performance rocket so far disclosed, with a maximum velocity of 2.5 km/sec (5,700 m.p.h.).

The rocket (see Plate 1) weighs four tons fully loaded, of which three are fuel (alcohol and oxygen) so that the mass ratio is four. (With a very small payload, it may be over 4.5) The propellants are all burnt in 75 seconds, being forced into the motor by a small turbine-pump driven by super-heated steam obtained, as in V.2, from decomposing hydrogen peroxide. The exhaust velocity is about 2.3 km/sec, which from Equation III.2 indicates a maximum speed for the rocket of 3.2 km/sec, but some 20 per cent of this is lost against air-resistance and gravity.

The rocket's calculated performance curves [4] are reproduced in Figure 6 as they show very clearly the characteristics of any such high-altitude machine. The points

[4] These curves are based on the first design study of "Viking"; the final results may differ from them in detail.

which should be noted are: (1) the fact that the thrust rises by some 10 per cent. as the rocket leaves the atmosphere and the motor, now operating in a near-vacuum, becomes more efficient; (2) the decrease in air-drag above 7 kms altitude, and the resulting rapid increase in acceleration past this point to a final value (when the almost empty machine is under maximum thrust) of over $10g$; (3) the fact that when the fuel is exhausted, the rocket has only risen a fraction of its ultimate height—its velocity now being sufficient for it to "coast" upward for more than 300 kms before coming to rest and falling back to Earth.

All these features will be observed, to a greater or lesser extent, in the performance of any rocket leaving the Earth, although considerably smaller final accelerations would be used in a large machine.

"Viking" is also of interest as it employed for the first time types of control which may play an important part in spaceship design. A rocket can be steered in space only by the use of its motors to give a lateral thrust. In V.2 this was done by small graphite "rudders" in the exhaust, and these were a source of frequent trouble. In "Viking", however, the entire motor can be tilted slightly to alter the line of thrust. The rocket is moreover fitted with small tangential jets (operated by the exhaust steam from the turbine) which can correct for roll around the longitudinal axis. The use of such auxiliary jets foreshadows similar applications on spaceships and space stations, and will be discussed in more detail in Chapter VIII. By their use, it is clearly possible for any type of manoeuvre to be carried out in three dimensions.

For further information on the practical details and engineering aspects of rocket design, the reader is referred

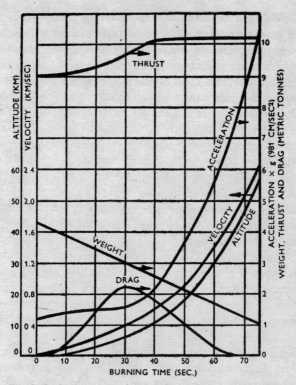

Fig. 6. Performance curves for high-altitude liquid-propellant rocket.

to the bibliography and to the *Journals* of the American
Rocket Society and the British Interplanetary Society.

Single-stage rockets of the same general design as
"Viking", with steadily improved motors and higher mass-
ratios, will be intensively developed for scientific research
during the next decade. They will eventually reach heights

of several thousand miles—a tremendous achievement by present standards but still a small one when set against the goal of interplanetary flight. Nevertheless, the information they will bring back from space, and the practical experience they will teach, will be essential before any plans can be made for more ambitious projects.

Chapter IV

THE PROBLEM OF ESCAPE BY ROCKET

Velocity Requirements

THE GROUND covered in the last two chapters now enables us to discuss, in a quantitative manner, the problem of escape from the Earth by rocket. We have seen that if a body can attain a speed of more than 11.2 km/sec (or less if it is already at a great height) then it will travel away from the Earth indefinitely with no further expenditure of power. And we have seen how to calculate the final velocity reached by a rocket after combustion of its fuel.

Equation III.2, on which our previous calculations were based, was however, derived for the theoretical case of a rocket acted upon by no forces except its own exhaust. A machine rising in the Earth's atmosphere will experience two retarding forces which may be considerable—air resistance, and the downward pull of gravity. The corrected equation for the rocket's final velocity after a vertical ascent (at the moment of fuel cut-off) must therefore be written

$$V = c \, \log_e R - gt - V_D \qquad \ldots \qquad \ldots \qquad (IV.1)$$

where t is the time of flight and V_D is the total velocity loss due to air-drag. The acceleration of gravity, g, is of course assumed to be constant during the period of powered ascent: this is nearly true in most cases that are likely to occur, for a rocket would burn most of its fuel while still relatively near the Earth.

It is quite impossible to give a general formula for the air-resistance loss: it depends on the shape and size of the rocket, the acceleration characteristics of its path, and the height of take-off. Since a high-velocity rocket spends only a short part of its powered trajectory in the relatively dense lower atmosphere, it does not reach considerable speeds until the air is already very rarefied, and towards the end of the burning period air-drag is quite negligible. (See Figure 6). Very small rockets, which are more affected by air-resistance because of their proportionally greater surface-area, may derive considerable advantage from being launched at great heights (e.g. from mountain tops) so that they begin their powered flight in air which is already of reduced density. This expedient is not necessary for rockets of any size[1], and for very large machines air-resistance may be neglected in the calculations. On a spaceship the velocity loss due to air-drag would be less than 1 per cent. of the calculated terminal speed: even on the four-ton "Viking" it is only about 7 per cent. as shown in the table below, (calculated for an ascent with 100 lb payload).

				m/sec
Actual velocity at all-burnt	...	...	...	2,500
Gravitational loss	...	...	...	750
Air-drag loss	...	...	...	250
Calculated all-burnt velocity	...	...	...	3,500

Considerably more important, it will be noticed, is the gravitational loss term gt. Since this depends directly

---

[1] It may however sometimes be worthwhile to enable the motors to operate at higher efficiency than for a sea-level take-off.

on the time of operation of the motors, it can be reduced only by short burning times *and hence high accelerations*. The maximum acceleration which a large rocket can employ is, however, limited by the thrust of its motors. At take-off, when it was fully loaded, V.2 had an acceleration of only $1g$ and the value for "Viking" is about the same. (The leisurely ascent of a giant rocket invariably surprises those who are only acquainted with the common or back-garden variety, with their accelerations of $50g$ or more). When the propellant is nearly exhausted, liquid-fuel rockets may reach accelerations of about $10g$ unless the motor thrust is reduced. For manned rockets, such "throttling back" might be desirable, though as mentioned in Chapter IX a properly protected man can tolerate higher linear accelerations than it would be practical to stress a large machine to withstand.

In order to reach escape velocity, therefore, thrust periods of several minutes would be required—and each minute of vertical ascent means a loss to gravity of 0.6 km/sec or 1,300 m.p.h. This would be a very serious matter, but fortunately substantial savings can be effected by using non-vertical departure curves— "synergic curves", as will be explained later.

Since any rocket escaping from the Earth's neighbourhood must reach 11.2 km/sec, we can substitute this constant value in Equation III.2.a. and see how the mass-ratio R varies with the assumed exhaust velocity c. The equation—ignoring "gravitational loss" for the moment— then becomes

$$R = e^{\frac{11.2}{c}}$$

Neglecting gravitational loss assumes that the rocket's acceleration is infinite ($t=0$) and this limiting case is shown by the curve $n=\infty$ in Figure 7. It will be seen that

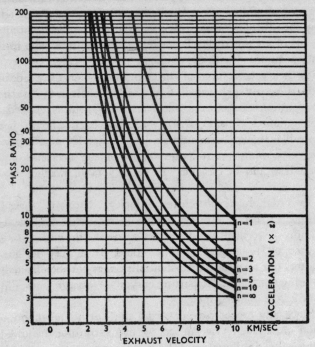

Fig. 7. *Mass-ratio curves for escape from the Earth, at various accelerations.*

with the best present-day fuels (c less than 2.5 km/sec) a mass-ratio of about 100 would be required—about ten times the limit that is practicable even with a very small pay-load.

When exhaust velocities of around 4.5 km/sec are available, which should be the case when the high-energy fluorine-based fuels can be handled, the mass-ratio necessary would be reduced to rather more than 10. This is still too high a value, thus confirming the conclusion already reached in the last chapter that it is impossible to build a single-stage, chemically-propelled rocket to escape from the Earth, even with no payload.

When one allows for the gravitational loss caused by the rocket's finite acceleration, the picture is even blacker. Assuming that the rocket maintains a constant acceleration of ng (where n is not likely to exceed values of 5 to 10) it is easy to show (see Appendix) that the required mass-ratio for escape is given by the increased value

$$R_n = e^{\frac{11.2}{c} \frac{n+1}{n}} = R^{\frac{n+1}{n}} \qquad \qquad \dots \quad \text{(IV.2)}$$

This function has been plotted in Figure 7 for various values of n, and the enormous losses incurred when n is low will be readily seen. The *reductio ad absurdum* case occurs when $n=0$, and the rocket has merely enough thrust to hang motionless in the air above its launching site until the fuel is exhausted!

Figure 7 will repay careful study, since it shows at one and the same time the paramount importance of high exhaust velocities and high accelerations. If a 10 km/sec fuel were available, the problem of building a single-stage rocket to reach escape velocity would be relatively easy. For a rocket accelerating at $5g$, the mass-ratio required would be less than 4, whereas with present propellants the figure would be about 200.

The above discussion is quite valid as far as it goes and

has been used by many to prove that space-flight must remain impossible. There are, however, few cases in scientific history of "negative predictions" surviving the passage of time. When, *taking all factors into account*, anything can be proved to be impossible, that usually means that it will be done in some different manner and employing a new and unforeseen technique. Demonstrations of the impossibility of heavier-than-air flight (a popular recreation among conservative scientists at the end of the last century) overlooked the petrol engine: those who believed that atomic power would never be released did not imagine the self-sustaining chain reaction and the ubiquitous neutron.

Much of technological progress consists of pincer movements around insoluble problems which eventually become left so far behind that their very existence is forgotten. In the case of astronautics, two solutions were put forward to overcome the difficulties discussed above. The first accepted the need for very high mass-ratios and proposed a method of construction—the step-rocket—which made them engineering possibilities. The second was much more daring: it proposed that the escape from Earth should not take place in one stage, but in two or more, the rocket actually being refuelled in space. This technique of orbital refuelling not only makes possible reductions in the overall masses required for interplanetary voyages, but, as we shall see later, opens up a whole range of important subsidiary projects.

These are not the only solutions: the third and most significant of all was revealed to the world with the explosion of the first atomic bomb. The subject of nuclear propulsion for spaceships is, however, of sufficient importance and complexity to demand a chapter in itself.

The Step-Rocket

Once one has, by careful design, constructed a rocket with the maximum possible value of mass-ratio, increasing the overall size of the machine will merely scale-up the ultimate payload in the same proportion: nothing can be done, on these lines, to increase the final speed. If, however, the payload is itself a second, smaller but self-contained rocket, which can now be separated from the empty lower component, the final speed can obviously be doubled. Indeed, the performance could be better than this, for the second rocket would start with several advantages—not the least being that it was already in a vacuum, and its motor would therefore operate at maximum efficiency.

This is the principle of the step-rocket, which may, in theory, be carried to any number of stages. If all the steps are identical in mass-ratio and motor-performance, then n steps would enable the last component to travel n times as fast as any single-stage rocket. It should thus be possible to escape from the Earth, even with present fuels, with a rocket of three or more steps.

The step principle is of fundamental importance, but its limitations are obvious—for the mass of each successive stage increases until enormous take-off values are reached. To quote a simple example, a modern high-performance rocket with a mass-ratio of 4 would have a weight-distribution not far from these figures:—

Payload	...	...	...	5%
Structure	...	...	...	20%
Fuel ...	...	...	...	75%
				100%

Since each rocket forms the payload of the step beneath it, the steps would increase in mass by a factor of 20. A three-step machine of total mass 400 tons would thus have a final payload of only 100 lbs (50 kg), which would achieve a speed of 3 $\log_e 4$ or about 4.15 times the exhaust velocity of the propellants employed.

This would still be insufficient to escape from the Earth with present fuels, though it should be possible with propellants and motors available in the quite near future (if not already in undisclosed use). A detailed analysis by Malina and Summerfield [2] indicates that a five-step rocket burning oxygen and hydrogen and with an initial mass of only 40 tons could take 100 lbs away from the Earth—an indication of how exceedingly sensitive performance figures are to improvements in exhaust velocity. A five-step oxy-alcohol rocket with the same payload would need an initial mass of over 500 tons.

It is not absolutely essential—though it is preferable—that the successive stages in a step-rocket be of geometrically increasing sizes: they can, indeed, be all of comparable mass, the most important requirement being that each is jettisoned as soon as its work is done, so that no "dead-weight" is carried a moment longer than necessary. The first step-rocket of any size—the solid fuel, 140-mile-range missile "Rheinbote", [3] illustrated in Plate IV, consisted of four steps of only slowly diminishing size (695, 425, 395 and 200 kg respectively).

If the step-rocket is taken to its logical conclusion, one arrives at a design with almost infinite subdivision, as in the

[2] *Journal of the Aeronautical Sciences*, **14**, 471, August 1947.
[3] Used operationally by the Germans on a very small scale in the closing months of the War.

"cellular" spaceship proposed by the British Interplanetary Society in 1938. (See page 94). This involved the use of about two thousand solid-propellant motors, each quite self-contained, arranged in a sort of honey-comb which disintegrated layer by layer as the fuel was burnt and the empty "cellules" were discarded. In this way it appeared possible to build a rocket with an initial mass of a thousand times the final mass. Owing to the added structural material, however, this would not give the mass-ratio of 1000 which might at first sight be expected, but a much smaller effective value—though one still high enough, it was hoped, to make the lunar journey possible with chemical propellants.

The first liquid-fuel step-rocket was fired in February 1949 when a composite unit consisting of a German V.2 carrying an American "WAC Corporal" was launched at White Sands, New Mexico (See Plate V). Although this was something of an improvisation, it was successful, as the upper component reached an altitude of 400 kms (250 miles) and a velocity of 2.3 km/sec (5,000 m.p.h.) It is interesting to compare these figures with the speeds and altitudes attainable by the components individually.

	Max. velocity (km/sec)	Max. altitude kms
WAC Corporal [4]	1.2	70
V.2	1.6	185
WAC + V.2 ...	2.3	400

There is a rather striking analogy between the step-principle and the technique used in polar expeditions, such as Scott's, in the days before air-transportation. A fairly large body of men would carry as much food and stores as

[4] As the WAC Corporal is normally launched by a large booster rocket, its "unassisted" performance would be poorer than this.

possible to an advanced base and would return, leaving a smaller group to "take-off" from this point, and if necessary the process would be repeated again at a later stage.

At the end of the war the Germans were considering the design of a two-step rocket of transatlantic range using a winged V.2 (known as A.9) as its upper component. The lower step or "booster" (A.10) would have had a mass of almost 100 tons. This project never materialized, but something of the sort is undoubtedly one of the next developments in large-scale rocket research. An A.10+V.2+WAC Corporal three-step combination would enable heights of over 1,000 kms to be reached with present-day fuels.

The use of step-rockets involves a number of technical difficulties, of which one of the most serious is the mechanical complexity introduced. Another is the possible danger caused by large quantities of expended rocketry descending from the skies, but this may not be of great importance since all rocket launching sites are of necessity well away from civilization. However, since the burned-out steps would represent very valuable equipment which could be used again, strenuous efforts would be made to retrieve them in good condition, and parachute braking might be used, as indeed was intended by the Germans for A.10. A better solution would be to convert the empty steps into lightly-loaded gliders which could be automatically steered back to the launching site.

It is difficult to say what the ultimate limits to the size and hence speed of step-rockets are likely to be. If one was prepared to build a multi-stage machine with an initial mass equal to that of the "Queen Mary" (but costing a good deal more) it might be possible, even with chemical fuels, to make a manned circumnavigation of the Moon.

But the difficulty and expense of the project would be so enormous that it must be regarded as unlikely. At the best, it could only be done at rare intervals as a stupendous engineering operation that would tax the resources of a wealthy country. Flights to the other planets, or an actual landing on the Moon, would be out of the question by such means. The situation, however, would become much more favourable if "orbital techniques" were employed.

Orbital Refuelling

We have seen in Chapter II that it is much easier for a body to enter a closed, stable orbit round a planet than to escape from it entirely—the necessary velocities near the Earth being about 8 and 11 km/sec respectively. Let us therefore suppose that it is possible to build rockets capable of reaching orbital speed with small payloads. (This could easily be done by two-step rockets when fuels of the 4 km/sec class are available). Then let us suppose that many rockets, all carrying fuel as their payload, are projected up into the same orbit. Although all the machines would have velocities of some 18,000 m.p.h. relative to the Earth's surface, they would be at rest with respect to one another and could, in principle at least, be coupled together so that all the fuel could be transferred to one machine. This procedure may sound fantastic, but since all the rockets would be travelling together in an unresisting vacuum, it would be in many ways simpler than the problem of flight-refuelling in air. Some of the technical difficulties involved, and their possible solutions, will be considered in the chapter on "space-stations".

43

One of the rockets is now refuelled, and, moreover, is circling the Earth, in space, at a speed of 8 km/sec. *It thus needs only an additional 3 km/sec to reach escape velocity and leave the Earth completely.* This technique would enable circumnavigations of the Moon to become practicable and might even open up the possibility of journeys (without landing) to the nearer planets.

By breaking down the task into two portions, therefore, we have greatly simplified the problem and are now faced with the task, not of launching a single enormous rocket weighing perhaps 50,000 tons, but a large number of rockets whose individual masses would be a few hundred tons. This would still be a tremendous undertaking and the *total* masses would be very great. However, it is at least an order of magnitude simpler than the first alternative.

This procedure was first investigated in great detail by the Austrian engineer Count von Pirquet in the late 1920's. Von Pirquet was concerned largely with the problem of escape from Earth but as we shall see later this technique may play an equally important part in other missions.

Before leaving the subject for the present, it may be instructive to consider what orbital refuelling means in terms of the Earth's gravitational "pit" (Figure 2.) It implies that, instead of having to climb out of the 4,000-mile-deep valley in a single exertion, we can rest and recuperate halfway up the slope, and continue the journey again when convenient. Equally important, the same procedure can be adopted on the return.

Finally, there are two other factors which make the orbital procedure of outstanding significance. A rocket taking off from the Earth's equator already has a tangential velocity, due to rotation, of 0.46 km/sec—a contribution towards orbital speed which is not to be despised. Secondly, if instead of climbing vertically until escape velocity is reached, the rocket turns as quickly as possible toward the horizontal (outside the atmosphere, of course) the greater part of the gravitational loss term in Equation IV.1 can be avoided. Gravity can only reduce the *vertical* component of the rocket's speed: it cannot affect the tangential or horizontal component—which in this case is the important one. If one could imagine a vast horizontal launching-track along which the rocket could accelerate at ground level until circular (or even escape) velocity was reached, there would be no gravitational loss at all. Since air-resistance as well as engineering economics makes this impossible there must be some loss while the rocket climbs out of the atmosphere, but it can be reduced to a relatively small value.

The optimum departure curve—initially vertical and curving towards the horizontal at a height of about a hundred kilometers—was investigated by Oberth, who called it the "synergic curve". Its employment, instead of the more obvious vertical ascent, makes possible very substantial reductions of mass ratio.

Chapter V

THE EARTH-MOON JOURNEY

Velocity Requirements

THE SIMPLEST of all journeys into space, and the first which will be actually accomplished, is the journey to or around the Moon, which will now be considered in detail. The conclusions reached in this chapter will apply, it should be noted, both to guided missiles, uncontrolled projectiles, or manned spaceships. They must all obey the same fundamental laws.

As far as energy requirements are concerned, Figure 2 shows that the Moon is, dynamically speaking, very nearly at "infinity", despite its astronomical nearness. It needs a velocity of 11.2 km/sec to project a body to infinity—and 11.1 km/sec to project it so that it just reaches the Moon (385,000 kms or 240,000 miles at mean distance). This velocity difference is so small that it is frequently ignored and it is assumed that the full escape velocity is needed for the mission.

A body leaving the Earth in the direction of the Moon would be subject to the gravitational field of both bodies, but for three-quarters of the way that of the Moon is completely negligible, as is shown in Figure 8. This diagram gives the accelerations produced by Earth and Moon in cm/sec^2: in order to show the values over the region where both are significant, the scale here has been multiplied by 100.

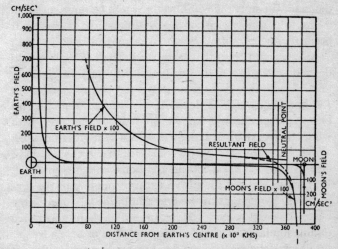

Fig. 8. Gravitational fields of Earth and Moon.

Since the fields are opposing, they have been drawn on opposite sides of the horizontal axis, and it will be seen that there is a point—the so-called "neutral point"—at which both fields are equal and the resultant (represented by the dotted line) vanishes. Up to this point the body would have an acceleration towards the Earth: thereafter, the force acting upon it would be directed to the Moon. It might be mentioned here that, contrary to the vivid descriptions given by many writers, absolutely *no* physical phenomena of any kind would take place in a rocket passing this point. Since the machine would be in a "free fall", with only gravitational forces acting upon it, its occupants would be weightless and so would be quite unaware of the fact that the actual direction of fall had altered. Nor would it be possible for a body with insufficient speed to be stranded at

47

the neutral point: the equilibrium would be quite unstable owing to the movement of the Moon and the (very small) perturbations produced by the Sun and planets.

As it receded from the Earth the rocket's velocity would decrease according to the escape-velocity curve in Figure 1, and it would thus pass the neutral point at a speed of about 1.6 km/sec in its fall towards the Moon. The Moon's escape velocity is 2.34 km/sec, and this is the speed with which the rocket, if it started from rest at a great distance, would crash into the Moon's surface. In the case we have taken the rocket has a certain additional energy since it left Earth with a speed slightly in excess of minimum requirements. Allowing for this, we find that in the fall towards the Moon it would reach a terminal speed of about 2.8 km/sec (6,300 m.p.h.). Clearly, if a safe landing is to be made, this speed must be neutralized by the further application of rocket power.

Obviously this is not quite the most economical journey to the Moon as the spaceship did not crawl past the "neutral point" but went through it at an appreciable speed—in other words, it started with more than the minimum velocity needed for the mission. This excess speed carried over from the original take-off would increase the difficulty of the lunar landing, and a small saving would be made if the rocket left Earth with barely enough speed to reach the neutral point. The initial velocity would then be 11.1 instead of 11.2 km/sec, and it would reach the Moon at 2.34 instead of 2.8 km/sec—a total reduction of, surprisingly enough, as much as 0.6 km/sec for the mission.

There is an infinite number of possible trajectories to the Moon, according to the initial velocity and direction of the rocket when leaving the Earth: but in every case it must reach the Moon at a speed of not less than 2.34 km/sec unless some form of braking is employed. To return again to the analogy of the two adjacent valleys in Figure 2, this is the speed which the rocket will acquire in falling into the upper of the two pits if it has just sufficient energy to surmount the "hump" between them.

If the rocket was not falling directly towards the Moon, but *past* it, then it would go round our satellite in an approximately parabolic or hyperbolic orbit and in certain cases might return to Earth. The exact shape of the orbits near the Moon is very sensitive to small changes in the initial velocity and direction: according to Kooy and Uyten-bogaart[1] all the possible "return" orbits lie within a speed range of only 1 per cent. at the projection point, i.e. between about 11.1 and 11.2 km/sec. Below 11.1 km/sec it would be impossible to reach the Moon: above 11.2 km/sec the body would be travelling too fast, when it passed the Moon, for our satellite to deflect it back to Earth.

Just as the Earth has its characteristic circular velocity of about 8 km/sec, so has the Moon, the value for a point near its surface being 1.65 km/sec (equivalent to a period of 1.8 hours). It may seem a little odd to speak of satellites of satellites, but from the point of view of the Sun this is what the Moon already is! If, therefore, when a rocket was falling past the Moon its speed was reduced to the appropriate value by firing its motors in the direction of flight, then it might continue to circle our satellite, perhaps taking observations automatically and radioing them back to Earth. If the fuel reserves were sufficient, it might at a later time be accelerated again into an orbit which would return it

[1] *Ballistics of the Future*, p. 457.

to our planet. The velocities on the return journey would be identical with those on the outward one: the rocket would cross the neutral point at its minimum speed, and then accelerate more and more rapidly until it reached the Earth at 11.1 km/sec—the speed with which it originally started.

It will be seen, therefore, that as soon as it becomes possible to build rockets which can escape from the Earth at all, a considerable range of interesting possibilities will be opened up. The payloads of the first "parabolic" rockets will be only a few kilograms and they will herald their arrival on the Moon by the flash they produce in our telescopes. According to Goddard, less than three pounds of flash-powder would cause an explosion easily visible in quite a small instrument. Later it will be possible to employ considerably larger payloads and light-weight radio transmitters, relaying the information obtained by arrays of recording instruments, will be installed. Finally, it will be possible to use television to obtain close-ups of the Moon, and, in particular, of its far side which can never be seen from Earth.

These later developments will require improvements in telemetering and telecontrol equipment almost as great as in rocket motor design, but do not demand anything essentially novel. The subject of radio links over astronomical distances will be discussed in a later chapter: in any case, it may safely be assumed [2] that propulsion and guiding techniques will advance together and that when we can build a rocket capable of reaching the Moon we will also be able to control it at that point.

The above discussion leads us to the conception of the

[2] Even by the disheartened rocket engineer who made the celebrated remark "The trouble with guided missiles is that there aren't any".

"characteristic velocity" which a rocket needs if it is to carry out any particular mission. For a rocket which is required to reach the Moon, but may be allowed to crash on it unchecked or shoot past it into space, this velocity, as we have seen, is 11.1 km/sec, or a little less than the velocity of escape. If it is desired to make a landing to set down instruments or, later, human beings, then the machine's fall into the Moon's field must be counteracted. This means that in some way the rocket must be reorientated in space so that its motors point towards the Moon, and rocket braking must be employed. To put it picturesquely, the rocket must "sit on its exhaust" and so descend slowly on to our satellite's surface.

If this manoeuvre was carried out in the most economical manner possible, it would require the combustion of exactly as much fuel as the *escape* from the Moon. Both missions are identical apart from the change in sign: it requires just as much energy to accelerate in space as to decelerate. The Moon's escape velocity being 2.34 km/sec, the characteristic velocity for the whole trip is 11.1+2.34 or 13.44 km/sec. The rocket must therefore be designed as if it had to reach this speed, and this is the figure which must be substituted in Equation III.2.a to obtain the mass-ratio required for the mission. The rocket, of course, never reaches this speed, since it divides its efforts between the two ends of the voyage: however, it would be capable of doing so if it burnt its fuel in one prolonged burst.

Mass Ratio Requirements

This figure of nearly 13.5 km/sec is a theoretical minimum value: it does not allow for gravitational loss at the take-off from Earth and an exactly corresponding, though much smaller, loss at the lunar landing. Taking these factors into account, the characteristic velocity for a voyage from rest on the Earth's surface to rest on the Moon's is about 16 km/sec (36,000 m.p.h.) With the most powerful chemical fuels ever likely to be available this would require an effective mass-ratio of about 35 and hence would involve the use of rockets of at least three stages, or else the orbital refuelling techniques mentioned before.

For a return journey the characteristic velocity must be doubled: it would therefore be about 32 km/sec. However, an interesting and important complication arises here. The descent on to the Moon could only be carried out by rocket braking, since there is practically no atmosphere. In the case of the Earth, the final landing could certainly be by parachute or some equivalent aerodynamic means. Indeed, it is possible that the greater part of the 11.1 km/sec which the rocket would acquire on its long fall back from the neutral point could be destroyed by air-resistance, by the technique of "braking ellipses."

This procedure was worked out in great detail by the early German writers and is as follows. Suppose that in its fall towards the Earth the rocket is aimed so that it passes through the highest levels of the atmosphere—at an altitude of about 100 kilometers. It will suffer a certain amount of retardation due to air-resistance, which, if the altitude is chosen correctly, can be of any desired value. (There would be no great danger of the rocket becoming incandescent at these altitudes, for it would have only one-fifth of the speed of a meteor at this level and the air-resistance would therefore be only a twenty-fifth as great). After "grazing" the atmosphere, the rocket would again emerge into space, where the frictional heating produced on its walls could be lost by radiation. It would now, however, be travelling at a speed substantially less than escape velocity, and so after receding from Earth to a considerable distance would return again along a very elongated ellipse. At "perigee" it would re-enter the atmosphere, cutting through it at a lower level but at less speed than on the first contact.

In this way, after a series of diminishing ellipses, the rocket could shed most of its excess speed without using any fuel. Indeed, it has been calculated that the entire landing on the Earth could be carried out in this manner, the final "touch-down" being by parachute. Before this can be settled definitely much more extensive knowledge of the upper atmosphere will be required, but undoubtedly substantial savings of fuel can be effected in this way.

Taking the most optimistic view we can calculate the "characteristic velocity" for the round trip as follows:—

	Theoretical minimum	Allowing for "g-loss"
Escape from Earth ...	11.1	12.5
Landing on Moon	2.34	3.0
Take-off from Moon ...	2.34	3.0
Navigational corrections	—	0.5
	15.78 km/s	19.0 km/s

The more pessimistic estimate, which assumes that the whole of the landing on Earth would have to be done by rocket braking, would be about 32 km/sec.

These performances would demand effective mass-ratios of about 70 and 1,000 respectively with the best conceivable chemical fuels, from which it will be seen what an important role air-braking can play if it proves practicable. But even the lower figure of 70 would require, for a ship large enough to carry men and their equipment, an initial mass of many thousand tons at take-off. This demonstrates once again the virtual impossibility of a return voyage to the Moon, with landing, in a chemically-propelled rocket.

The economics of the Earth-Moon voyage would, however, alter drastically if orbital refuelling was employed. There are many ways in which this might be done, and a recent scheme [3] will be described as an example of one such method.

Instead of launching a single mammoth rocket, which might have to weigh 20,000 tons or so, *three* rockets each of about 600 tons mass would take off simultaneously and enter an orbit 500 miles from the Earth. Two would merely act as "tankers" and would refuel the third, which would then accelerate out of its orbit and travel towards the Moon. On reaching the vicinity of the Moon, it would enter a circular orbit around our satellite at an altitude of a few hundred miles, *and would here detach the fuel tanks needed for the return journey*. These would be left circling the Moon while the ship descended to the surface.

When it took off again, it would rendezvous on to the still orbiting fuel tanks, reattach them, and make the return journey to Earth. The beauty of this scheme—which could have several other variations—is that no unnecessary work would be done and hence a vast saving in overall weight could be effected. Instead of carrying the fuel for the return journey and final Earth landing down to the Moon and up again, it would be left in space where it could be

[3] H. E. Ross, "Orbital Bases": *J.B.I.S.*, 8, 4-7, Jan. 1949.

collected on the homeward voyage. This would save decelerating several tons of fuel from 2 km/sec down to zero and re-accelerating it from zero up to 2 km/sec again.

The technical difficulties involved in this sort of manoeuvre would of course be considerable, and a single mistake at any stage might be fatal. But it must be remembered that once a body is set circling in an orbit, its position for many years ahead can be predicted with great accuracy, so the location of the fuel "caches" would always be known with precision. Moreover, as we shall see in Chapter IX, the very smallest of radio beacons would enable them to be located at a range of thousands of miles in free space.

It must also be realized that such an enterprise would not be carried out *de novo*, but only after a long period of experimentation when earlier expeditions had made numerous circumnavigations of the Moon and perhaps already established orbital fuel reserves.

The main assumption in such schemes as this is that the problems of navigation and control of large rockets will be solved as completely as for aircraft, and there seems no reason to suppose that this will not be the case. These are subjects to which we will return when discussing spaceships and space-stations.

Transit Times

So far, no mention has been made of the duration of the lunar journey. If the rocket maintained its initial speed of 11 km/sec (25,000 m.p.h.) it would reach the Moon after 10 hours, but since its velocity is steadily decreasing the figure is considerably greater. For a body leaving the Earth's neighbourhood at the minimum speed which enables it to reach the Moon at all (11.1 km/sec), the journey to the Moon's orbit takes about 116 hours (see Appendix, Equation V.1). This, however, ignores the acceleration of the Moon's field towards the end of the journey, which would produce a small but appreciable reduction of transit time.

This figure of 116 hours is therefore the *maximum* length of time a free projectile could take on the direct journey to the Moon. A rocket which had to engage in retarding manoeuvres would, of course, be longer on the journey.

Five days is not a great deal of time in which to make a voyage to another world [4] and it would decrease very sharply if the rocket left the Earth with any appreciable excess speed over the minimum of 11.1 km/sec. (See Appendix, Equations V.2, 3) Some typical values for these transit times are tabulated below.

Table 2

Initial velocity km/sec	Transit time hours
11.1	116
11.2	49
12.2	19
13.2	14
14.2	11
15.2	10
16.2	8
21.2	6

These figures have been calculated for the mean distance of the Moon—385,000 kms or 240,000 miles—and would

[4] It compares quite favourably with the ten weeks of Columbus first voyage!

vary somewhat from time to time as the Moon's distance alters slightly: but they give a good idea of the order of duration of the journey under various conditions. The fact that doubling the initial speed reduces the transit time to a twentieth is certainly surprising, and is a good example of the danger of relying on ordinary terrestrial ideas of transport when discussing astronautics. However, speeds of 20 km/sec will still remain of purely theoretical interest for a long time after lunar journeys have become common-place, and the early explorers will no doubt prefer fairly leisurely journeys to give them ample time to check their position and carry out their somewhat intricate braking manoeuvres.

But no doubt in due course the survivors of the first generation of astronauts will shake their heads over the modern craze for speed, when the five days that was good enough for them begins to be carved down to five hours.

Chapter VI

INTERPLANETARY FLIGHT

The Sun's Gravitational Field

IN OUR discussion of lunar journeys in the last chapter, it was assumed that the Earth and Moon formed a more or less closed system and that the effects of other gravitational fields could be ignored. This is true, to a very high degree of accuracy, of the minute fields of the planets. The Sun's field, however, is far more powerful since it holds the Earth firmly in its orbit at a distance of over 90,000,000 miles, and it may well be asked if we were justified in ignoring it in our calculations.

To a first approximation the answer is—luckily—"yes". Although the Sun's influence is relatively large, its *variation* over the whole width of the Moon's orbit is very small—less than 1 per cent. of its absolute value. In other words, the Sun acts almost equally on Earth and Moon and on any object between them: a negligible error is therefore introduced if we ignore it completely. Its effect only appears in the third or later significant figures when more accurate calculations are required.

When we come to consider, not journeys from a planet to its nearby satellite, but from one planet to another, the situation is totally different. We must now alter our point-of-view from the Earth, holding its solitary Moon in its gravitational grip, to the Sun, keeping all the planets moving in its far more extensive field.

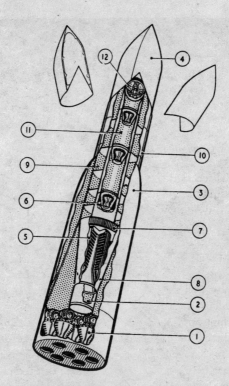

Plate VIII

"EXPENDABLE" SPACESHIP: *B.I.S. 1949*

Key to Principal Features:—

(1) Chemical booster—seven motors of 450 tons thrust, using liquid oxygen/liquid hydrogen. c assumed = 4 km./sec.

(2) Fuel for booster pumps.

(3)-(4) Expendable tanks for chemical booster.

(5) Atomic reactor: 1,100 tons thrust, using ammonia propellant. Weight, 40 tons. c assumed = 10 km./sec.

(6) Turbo-pump feed to reactor.

(7) Energy shielding—weight, 20 tons; density, 1 ton per metre^3.

(8) Gyro-regulated steering jets, incorporating steam exhaust from turbo-pumps.

(9) Expendable tanks for atomic propulsor.

(10) Jointed main longerons.

(11) Three-step chemical crew rocket, using liquid oxygen/liquid hydrogen. Weight, 60 tons, all-up. c assumed = 4 km./sec. (Serving also as health shielding during operation of atomic reactor—density, 6.25 tons per metre^3.)

(12) Pressurized crew chamber. Weight, 1.4 tons, including crew, instrumentation, provisions, etc.

Plate IX

Drawing by Leslie Carr

ORBITAL SPACESHIP BEING REFUELLED

Everything that has been said about the Earth's field in Chapter II applies, with a suitable alteration of scale, to the Sun's. At the surface of the Sun, the acceleration of gravity is 28 times that at the surface of the Earth. If we use this value for "g" and the appropriate value of the Sun's radius (695,500 kms or 432,000 miles) in the equations derived in the Appendix to Chapter II, we can find the magnitudes of the solar escape and circular velocities and the dimensions of the orbits for bodies moving in the Sun's field, exactly as we have done in the case of the Earth. We can also calculate the work needed to lift a body from the Sun's surface to infinity, and can express this in terms of a vertical distance—the "depth" of the Sun's gravitational pit. A comparison of the two sets of figures is instructive:—

	Earth	Sun
Escape velocity ...	11.2 km/sec	618 km/sec
Circular velocity	7.9 km/sec	437 km/sec
Equivalent depth of gravitational pit (1 g as standard)	6360 kms	19,500,000 kms

We are not, of course, concerned with leaving the actual surface of the Sun, but if we move from one planetary orbit to another we are required to move up or down the slope of the Sun's gravitational crater, which is precisely similar in shape to that of the Earth (Figure 2), except that it is 3,000 times as deep. It is therefore important to consider the locations of the Earth and planets on the slopes of this imaginary crater.

The usual scale-drawing of the Solar System, as found in most school atlasses and any astronomy book, shows the inner planets crowded round the Sun with the outer worlds at progressively increasing distances—up to 6,000,000,000 kms (3,750,000,000 miles) for Pluto, most distant of the Sun's children. The "energy diagram" of the system, however, presents a completely different picture. Far from being near the Sun in the gravitational sense, even the innermost planet, Mercury, is very remote from it. Whereas the full depth of the imaginary crater is nearly 20,000,000 kms, all the planets are crowded together on its very uppermost slopes, within 250,000 kms of the level plain into which it slowly flattens. This means that the work done in moving between the planetary orbits is only a small fraction of what it might well have been had the scale of the Solar System been different: indeed, we will presently see that crossing such an immense distance as that between Earth and Mars may require less energy than the journey between Earth and Moon.

In other words, the Sun's gravitational field, though of enormous extent, is very "flat" in the region of the planets and the climb up its slopes requires relatively little energy. Superimposed on this field are the much smaller fields of the individual planets. These are effective only over very short distances, but their gradients are relatively steep and so we have the paradox arising that the first thousand miles of an interplanetary journey may require more energy than the next score of millions. This state of affairs is depicted in Figure 9, which will be explained in more detail presently.

The planets, at their varying distances, are travelling round the Sun in orbits which are, in most cases, very nearly circular, and all are moving in the same direction and lie approximately in the same plane. The velocities of motion can be calculated from Equation II.8 with suitable values for the constants: they range from 48 km/sec in the case of

Mercury, the innermost planet, to 5 km/sec for Pluto, at the known limits of the Solar System. It will be seen, therefore that a body on any of the planets already possesses, by virtue of its orbital motion, a very large part of the energy needed for interplanetary voyages.

If we calculate, from Equations II.5 and II.8, the velocity of escape and the orbital velocity in the Sun's field at the position of the Earth, the values obtained are 42 and 30 km/sec respectively. The first figure is the velocity which a body, at rest in the Earth's orbit, would have to be given to project it past all the outer planets and far away from the Solar System—indeed, to the stars themselves, after many millions of years. The second figure is, of course, the velocity which the Earth already possesses: the difference (12 km/sec) is therefore the *additional* speed which must be imparted to a body, moving with the Earth but free of its gravitational field, to send it completely out of the Solar System. Since a velocity of 11 km/sec is needed to escape from the Earth itself, it therefore follows that a body given a *total* speed of 23 km/sec in the direction of the Earth's motion would leave not only our planet but also the Solar System.

Similar calculations can be made for all the other planets, and some of the results are shown in Figure 9. As far as the writer knows, this form of representation of the Solar System is due to Dr. R. S. Richardson, of Mount Wilson Observatory.

It will be seen that this drawing bears a considerable similarity to Figure 2, but whereas in the earlier diagram the ordinates were in terms of distance (and hence energy), here they are in the more convenient form of velocity. The diagram must be imagined as extending downwards

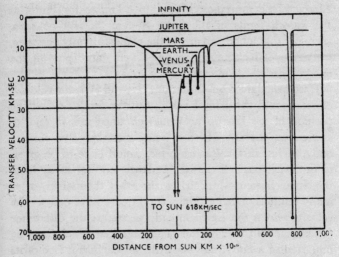

Fig. 9. Energy Diagram of the Solar System, in terms of Required Transfer Velocities.

ten times further than shown, to the 618 km/sec escape velocity needed to leave the actual surface of the Sun. The left-hand branch of the curve shows the additional "transfer velocity" needed by a body, already moving in a circular orbit round the Sun, to permit it to leave the Solar System. Even for the orbit of Mercury this additional velocity is only 20 km/sec—a very small fraction of the enormous values needed in the neighbourhood of the Sun.

On the right-hand side of the figure, the subsidiary escape velocity curves for the individual planets have been superimposed, so that the *total* velocity needed to leave the

Solar System from the surfaces of the five inner planets, and not merely from their orbits, may be seen at a glance.

A number of surprising facts emerges from this diagram, which will repay careful study. It is, for example, easier to leave the Solar System if one starts from Mercury than from Earth or Venus, although it is the nearest planet to the Sun. The most difficult spot to escape from in the entire system is the surface of Jupiter: from the energy point of view, it is much nearer the Sun than is Mercury!

Figure 9, it should be emphasised, does *not* show the velocities needed to get from one planet to another, but only those needed to escape from the combined fields of Sun and planet. But it does show the fact, which is of prime importance in interplanetary travel, that the energies needed to cross the great spaces of the Solar System are no more, and are often much less, than those needed to leave the planets themselves. A list of these latter values will be found in Table 6 (Chapter X).

Interplanetary Orbits

We will now consider the velocities required to make the interplanetary journey which is perhaps of the greatest interest—that from the Earth to Mars. The case examined will be that in which the maximum possible use is made of the planets' existing velocities. Obviously, if one had quite unlimited supplies of energy one could travel from one planet to another by any route one fancied, but for a long time to come only the orbits of minimum energy—the astronautical equivalents of great circle routes in terrestrial navigation—will be of practical interest.

Figure 10 (a) shows the orbits of the two planets drawn to scale, although as the orbit of Mars is actually somewhat eccentric (e=0.093) the average values of its radius and orbital speed have been taken for simplicity. This approximation will give results which are slightly too pessimistic for journeys when Mars is at its closest to the Sun, and vice versa, but the variations are very small.

The path of a spaceship in the Sun's controlling field must follow one of the curves—ellipse, parabola or hyperbola—discussed in Chapter II, and any of these could in principle be employed for interplanetary travel. But the path which, as will be almost intuitively obvious, is the easiest one to use is the ellipse which is tangent to both planetary orbits, and with the Sun at one focus.

It is easy to calculate, from Equation II.10, the velocity which a body needs to travel in such a path. When it was nearest the Sun, i.e. in the neighbourhood of the Earth, its speed would be 32.7 km/sec. As it grazed the orbit of Mars this would drop to 21.5 km/sec. These speeds do not differ very greatly from those of the planets themselves— 29.8 and 24.2 km/sec respectively.

To project a body, which is already moving in the Earth's orbit, out to Mars we need thus only give it an additional speed of 32.7—29.8 or less than 3 km/sec in the direction of the Earth's motion. It would then drift outwards away from the Sun along the ellipse of Figure 10 (a) until it reached the orbit of Mars. Its velocity would then be 24.2—21.5 or 2.7 km/sec too low for it to remain here and it would start to drop back to the Earth's orbit again. If, however, it was now given this "transfer" velocity of 2.7 km/sec it would remain in the Martian orbit. It could then land on Mars, using rocket braking against the planet's

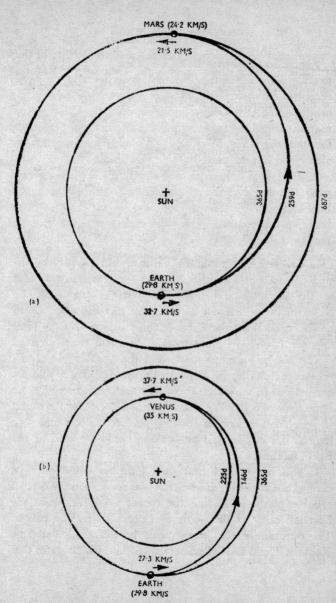

Fig. 10. *Cotangential orbits to Mars and Venus.*

gravitational field, or could become a third satellite of the little world, taking observations until it was time to start on the homeward voyage. The approximate "velocity budget" for the complete journey would thus be:—

		km/sec
Escape from Earth	...	11.2
Transfer to voyage orbit	...	2.9
Transfer from voyage to Mars orbit	...	2.7
Landing on Mars	...	5.0
Total	...	21.8

In practice this minimum value would have to be increased to about 25 km/sec to allow for gravitational losses at the landings and take-offs, course corrections, etc. Nevertheless, this is not such a large increase over the 16 km/sec needed for the Earth-Moon journey—yet the total distance covered is more than a thousand times greater!

The return journey, apart from the possible use of air-resistance braking in the Earth's atmosphere, would be carried out in an identical manner and would require the same total velocity. The characteristic velocity for the round trip would therefore be about 50 km/sec, or just under 40 km/sec if 100 per cent air-braking could be used at the Earth landing.

It will be realised that such journeys could only be carried out at the times when the planets were in the correct relative positions, so that the rocket would arrive at the Martian orbit at the point also occupied by the planet. The duration of the journey can be easily calculated by Kepler's Third Law of planetary motion, which states that the period in an elliptic orbit is proportional to the 3/2 power of its semi-major axis, *a*. If we express *a* in astronomical units—i.e. radii of the Earth's orbit—$a^{3/2}$ will thus give the complete period in years, and halving this will give the duration of the voyage. For the case quoted above (Mars at mean distance) the transit time is about 259 days, which is a considerable, but not an excessive duration. If the journey was made so as to reach Mars when it was nearest to the Sun the figure would be about 237 days, but the planetary configurations making this possible would be rather infrequent.

The minimum-energy or "cotangential" journey to Venus would be very similar, (Figure 10 (b)) except that in this case it would be necessary, once the rocket had escaped from the Earth, for it to *reduce* rather than increase its existing orbital velocity so that it would fall inwards towards the Sun. If the timing was correct, it would pass Venus in her orbit at a somewhat higher speed and would have to be slowed down to match her velocity. The figures for the complete journey would be:—

	km/sec
Escape from Earth ...	11.2
Transfer to voyage orbit ...	2.5
Voyage orbit to Venus orbit	2.7
Landing on Venus ...	10.4
Total	26.8

This is rather higher than for the Martian journey: the transit time is however much less—about 146 days.

On the above lines it is possible to calculate the "characteristic velocity" needed for any interplanetary journey, and a table of such values for the more important cases is given below.

Table 3

Mission	Theoretical velocity[1] km/s	Approximate Actual Velocity[2]	
		km/s	m.p.h.
One-way journeys			
Orbit round Earth	8	10	22,000
Escape from Earth	11.2	13	29,000
Earth to Moon	13.5	16	36,000
Earth to Mars	22	25	56,000
Earth to Venus	27	31	70,000
Return journeys			
Earth-Moon-Earth (no landing on Moon)	22.4	25	56,000
Lunar return trip (with landing on Moon)	27	32	72,000
Earth-Mars-Earth (no landing on Mars)	28	32	72,000
Mars return trip (with landing on Mars)	44	50	110,000
Earth-Venus-Earth (no landing on Venus)	28	32	72,000
Venus return trip (with landing on Venus)	54	62	140,000

[1] Ignoring air-resistance and gravitational loss.
[2] Including allowance for losses, but assuming no saving by air-resistance braking.

These values must be regarded as no more than approximations based on rather conservative assumptions, so that the actual values would certainly be somewhat less. No allowance has been made, for example, for the fact that a spaceship taking off from the Equator would possess an additional half a kilometer a second velocity owing to the Earth's rotation. And if, as some believe, the whole of the landing on Earth can be effected by air-braking alone, the figures for the return journeys would be reduced by 10 or 11 km/sec.

If this technique can be perfected for terrestrial landings, it will presumably be possible on Venus, which has an atmosphere at least as dense as Earth's; and a certain amount of braking may even be possible in the thin Martian air. The total velocity needed for the one-way journey to Venus would then be 16.4, not 26.8 km/sec, and for the return trip, about 32 instead of 53.6 km/sec.

The figures for the next longest interplanetary journey—that to Jupiter—are given below for comparison.

		km/sec
Escape from Earth		11.2
Transfer to voyage orbit ...		8.8
Transfer to Jovian orbit ...		5.7
Total		25.7

There would of course be no question of landing on Jupiter itself, since apart from the enormous energies this would require (see Figure 9) the planet probably possesses no solid crust and has several other singularly unattractive features which will be mentioned in Chapter X. But its system of at least eleven satellites is of considerable interest: several of them are worlds in their own right, much larger than the Moon and comparable in size to Mars. They could be visited, once the orbit of Jupiter had been reached, with relatively small expenditure of power, their escape velocities being 2 or 3 km/sec.

Unfortunately, the journey to Jupiter along the ellipse of minimum energy takes 2 years 9 months, and if manned voyages are to be made, faster orbits, requiring much higher velocities, would be necessary. They would be even more essential for journeys to the remote outer planets, which would last anything up to 45 years (for the one-way trip alone!) if cotangential paths were employed.

We have seen in Chapter II that there is an infinite number of ellipses and hyperbolae along which a body can travel in any gravitational field, if the initial velocities are suitably adjusted. Such trajectories, cutting sharply across the planetary orbits instead of grazing them as in the cases so far discussed, would be traversed in times much shorter than for the cotangential ellipse.

Some typical high-speed orbits are shown in Figure 11. As these not only involve greater velocities but much shorter distances than the minimum-energy voyages, the transit times would be reduced to small fractions of the former figures. Unfortunately, the energies needed for these orbits would be enormous, since they do not utilise the existing planetary velocities and very large projection speeds would be needed to force a body into one of them. Some of these orbits, for example, cut the Earth's almost at right angles, so that the whole of the Earth's 30 km/sec of velocity would have to be neutralised before a rocket could embark upon them. Such trajectories must therefore remain of theoretical interest only until space-flight has reached a fairly advanced technical stage.

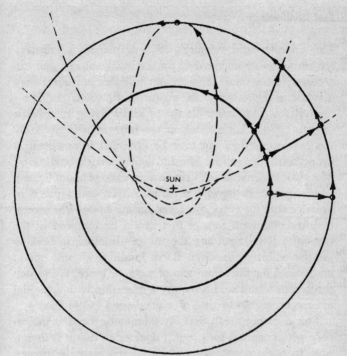

Fig. 11. Possible high-speed orbits.

If almost unlimited energy sources were available, it would be possible to travel from one planet to another in very nearly a straight line. The velocities required in this case would be of the order of a hundred kilometers a second, and the transit times to Mars or Venus would be less than a week. Such possibilities however, belong to the somewhat remote future, unless the technical developments discussed in the next chapter occur far more swiftly than even the most optimistic forecasts suggest.

Fuel Requirements

The characteristic velocities for interplanetary journeys are considerably higher than for the lunar voyage, and the necessary mass-ratios are very much higher still since they increase as the power of the characteristic velocity. (Equation III.2.a). Assuming the use of a fuel giving an exhaust velocity of 4.5 km/sec, which we have seen is probably the maximum that can ever be obtained from chemical propellants, the return Martian journey with landing on Mars would demand an effective mass-ratio of about 67,000, which is utterly beyond realization. (It would mean in practice that for every ton taken on the round trip several hundred thousand tons of fuel would be required at the take-off!) Even assuming the use of atmospheric braking for the whole of the final Earth landing, we still obtain mass-ratios for the round trip of 7,000 or more. Using step construction, this would require a spaceship with an initial mass comparable to that of a good-sized battle-fleet.

This does not mean that interplanetary travel is impossible with chemical fuels, but it does mean that it is impossible to build spaceships capable of reaching the planets from the Earth's surface, landing on them, and returning to the Earth *in a single operation*, carrying all the fuel for the complete mission. If the task could be broken down into its components, it would become easier by several orders of magnitude, and would enter the realm of engineering possibility. In other words, we are again compelled to consider orbital refuelling.

As an example of the sort of thing that might be done on these lines, consider a journey to Mars starting from an orbit around the Earth at a distance of 30,000 kms, the spaceship having been refuelled here as suggested in Chapter IV and described in more detail in Chapter VIII. It would then escape from this orbit and enter the cotangential ellipse taking it to Mars, the total velocity for this manoeuvre being about 4.4 km/sec. On approaching Mars and accelerating into its orbit, the ship would not land but would become a satellite of Mars at a distance of a few hundred kilometres from the surface. At this height it would be possible to learn an immense amount about the planet by telescopic observation.

The spaceship would continue to circle Mars in a free orbit until the planet was in the correct position for the return journey. This would involve a waiting period of 455 days, which, though long, means that it would be possible to observe a complete cycle of seasons over the two hemispheres. The total characteristic velocity for the mission would be as follows:—

	km/sec
Escape from orbit round Earth	1.5
Transfer to voyage orbit ...	2.9
Voyage orbit to Mars orbit	2.7
Entering orbit round Mars	1.5
Total	8.6

Assuming a rocket exhaust velocity of 4.5 km/sec, this could be accomplished with a mass-ratio of 7 or, for the return trip back into the orbit round Earth, 49. Such figures could be achieved by a spaceship of relatively few steps, the construction of which would be further simplified by the fact that it would never have to withstand high accelerations since it would always be operating in low gravitational fields. (This important point will be discussed again in Chapter VIII.) Although the complete project, including the fuelling of the ship in its orbit and the eventual retrieving of the crew by an auxiliary rocket when they had returned to the Earth's neighbourhood, would be exceedingly expensive and would require the combustion of hundreds of thousands of tons of fuel, there would never be any question of handling such quantities in a single operation or in a single machine. The largest amount to be dealt with at any one time would be a few thousand tons.

Numerous missions of a similar nature can be evolved on paper and could no doubt be realised in practice. Indeed, it may be assumed as fairly certain that the first reconnaissances of the planets will be by orbiting rockets which do not attempt a landing—perhaps expendable, unmanned machines with elaborate telemetering and television equipment. (The difficulty with a manned spaceship is that one has to get it back, and this involves squaring the mass-ratio!) It is even possible that landings on Mars might be effected by chemically-propelled rockets, if enough was discovered to make the crew's survival at all likely during the interval—certainly many years—before it became technically possible to take them off again.

As a more remote prospect, if the materials for refuelling spaceships could be found on any of the planets and extracted without undue difficulty, the economics of the entire project would change radically. (There would be little transatlantic flying even today if aircraft had to carry their fuel for the round trip.) But even when such co-operation makes it possible to budget for one-way trips only, and

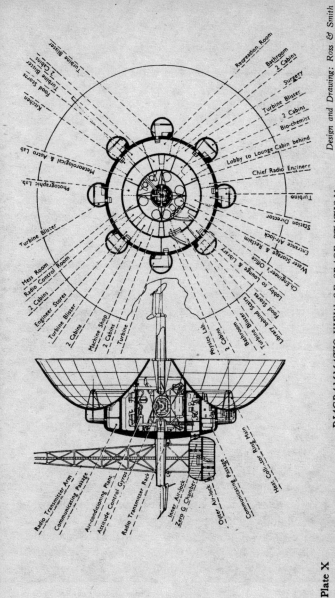

Recreation Room
Bathroom
2 Cabins
Surgery
Turbine Blister
2 Cabins
Bio-chemist
Lobby to Lounge Cabin behind
Chief Radio Engineer
Turbine
Station Director
Entrance Air-lock
Water Storage & Reclaim
Ch. Engineer's Office
Lobby to Lounge & Library
Food Stores
Library behind Stairs
Turbine Blister
Bathroom
2 Cabins
Physics Lab.

Turbine Blister
2 Cabins
Food Stores
Kitchen
Meteorological & Astro Lab.
Photographic Lab.
Turbine Blister
Mess Room
Radio Control Room
2 Cabins
Engineer Stores
Turbine Blister
2 Cabins
Machine Shop
2 Cabins
Turbine

Radio Transmitter Arm
Communicating Passage
Air-conditioning Plant.
Attitude Control Gyros.
Radio Transmitter Rack
Zero G Chamber
Inner Air-lock
Outer Air-lock
Communicating Passage
Hatch
Collar Ring Main

Design and Drawing: Ross & Smith

DIAGRAMMATIC VIEW OF SPACE STATION

Plate X

Plate XI

Design and Drawing: Ross & Smith

SPACE STATION.

even when orbital refuelling techniques are exploited to the utmost, flight to the other planets will remain a fabulously expensive enterprise, which can be carried out only at infrequent intervals. It would still be worth doing on purely scientific grounds and for the profounder reasons discussed in Chapter X: but even a flourishing world-state could not afford it very often.

All this is assuming that rocket exhaust velocities appreciably greater than 4.5 km/sec can never be attained. If this limitation can be circumvented in any way the whole picture will be altered. To take a specific case, consider the round trip to Mars which, as we have seen, requires a characteristic velocity of 50 km/sec if the mission is to be carried out as a single operation. The effective mass-ratios needed for this journey if high exhaust velocities can be obtained are listed below.

Exhaust velocity (km/sec)	4.5	5	7.5	10	15	20	25
Mass-ratio	67,000	22,000	790	148	28	12	7

The rate at which the figures decrease with relatively modest increases in exhaust velocity is astonishing. The value of exhaust velocity at which interplanetary travel begins to look a practical proposition rather than a prodigous scientific feat is about 10 km/sec—four times the value attainable today and twice that which seems the ultimate limit for chemically-propelled rockets. It is, therefore, natural to ask if such performances can be obtained by any application of atomic power.

It can be said at once that the energies released by nuclear reactions are of such a magnitude as to make the requirements of interplanetary travel look very modest indeed. At a very conservative estimate, the fifty or so pounds of fissile material in the first atomic bombs liberated 10,000,000 mile-tons of energy. This is more than sufficient to take a mass of 1,000 tons to the Moon *and* to bring it back to Earth—a feat which would require the combustion of millions of tons of chemical fuel. This fantastic dispropor-tion—50 pounds of plutonium doing the work of millions of tons of chemicals [3]—becomes even more astonishing when one considers that less than 0.1 per cent. of the total energy is actually liberated in present atomic explosions.

If even this 0.1 per cent. could be used to produce a propulsive jet, the "exhaust velocities" obtained would be about a thousand times those possible with chemical reactions. Instead of trying to design spaceships consisting of 90 per cent. fuel—and then having to discard section after section to get a sufficiently high final velocity—it would be quite literally true to say that the fuel was a com-pletely negligible fraction of the machine's mass—much less than 1 per cent. of the total.

This is certainly an attractive prospect after the rather depressing figures given earlier in this chapter. As we have now succeeded in liberating atomic energy both at con-trolled, low-energy and at uncontrolled, super-high energy levels, it may well be asked why so much time has been spent discussing the almost crippling limitations of chemical propellants, when atomic energy can open up not merely the nearer planets but the entire Solar System with equal ease.

[3] There is an apparent discrepancy here as it has been stated that the first atomic bomb was equivalent to 20,000 tons of T.N.T. But the greater part of the millions of tons mentioned above would be used merely to transport a smaller quantity of fuel out of the Earth's field: it is this factor which reduces still further the efficiency of the chemical fuel against the virtually weightless atomic fuel in this (highly theoretical) calculation.

The answer can be given at once. The controlled use of atomic energy is not going to be simple even for fixed generating stations with virtually no limitations of mass. And of all the possible uses of atomic energy, its application to aircraft and rocket propulsion appears the most difficult, and raises the most stubborn technical problems.

On the other hand, it is the one which offers the greatest dividends if it can be achieved. In its "terrestrial" applications atomic energy offers nothing essentially new. It can perform, perhaps more economically, what can also be done in other ways. But as a means of propulsion in space if offers —in theory at least—a solution to difficulties which would otherwise be totally insuperable.

When the time comes to write the history of atomic power and its impact on human affairs, it may well be found that all its other applications—countless though they may be—will be overshadowed by the fact that through its use Mankind obtained the freedom of space, with all that that implies.

Chapter VII

THE ATOMIC ROCKET[1]

Theoretical Basis

WE HAVE already seen that the only known method of propulsion in space is by means of reaction, and that if atomic power is to be used in astronautics it must be in some form of rocket. Undoubtedly it will differ radically from any type of rocket existing today, but as it must operate by producing a stream of matter moving at a high velocity in a narrowly defined jet, it does not seem inappropriate to retain the old name.

There appear, in principle, to be two main ways in which atomic energy can be employed to produce this effect. When a nuclear reaction takes place, the resulting products are ejected with extremely high velocities (about 10,000 km/sec for massive particles, and much more for electrons). If these velocities could be "channelized" into one direction then it would appear that enormous exhaust speeds would be available.

Unfortunately, it seems very difficult to do this, even in theory. The products of atomic reactions are ejected in random directions and cannot be "beamed" in the way that the expanding gas in the rocket combustion chamber is directed by the nozzle. It is true that any charged particles could be deflected in the required direction by magnetic

[1] Most of the material in this chapter has been obtained, with grateful acknowledgement, from four papers of the same title by L. R. Shepherd and A. V. Cleaver, *Journal of the B.I.S.*, Sept., Nov., 1948; Jan., March, 1949.

or electrostatic fields; but the fields required would be very great and could only be generated by impossibly heavy apparatus—which could not, of course, affect the heavier, uncharged particles at all.

Quite apart from this, there are fundamental reasons why such extremely high exhaust velocities (i.e. around 10,000 km/sec) could not be utilised even if it were possible to persuade all the products of a nuclear reaction to travel in the same direction. It is easy to show (see Appendix, Equation VIII.2) that the power generated in a rocket jet is 4,900 nc kilowatts per tonne, where n is the rocket's acceleration in gravities, and c is the exhaust velocity in km/sec. This means that, given two rockets of the same mass and acceleration, the rate of energy dissipated in the jet depends directly on its velocity.

A simple example may make clear the consequences of this. A V.2 rocket at the moment when its fuel is nearly exhausted has a mass of about 4 tonnes and $n=6$, approximately. Taking c as 2.25 km/sec, the total jet power is 265,000 kw or 355,000 H.P. This, it must be emphasised, is only the rate at which kinetic energy is going into the *jet*: the total power dissipation in the *motor* itself is several times as great owing to thermal inefficiencies. Inevitably a percentage of this energy will leak into the body of the rocket as heat and will raise its temperature slightly.

Now let us assume that we have a hypothetical atomically-powered V.2 with an exhaust velocity of a thousand times that of the alcohol-oxygen mixture. Its fuel consumption would thus be a thousand times less and it would need only a few kilograms of fuel to do the work of the eight tons of chemical propellant. Unfortunately, the rate of energy production in the jet would now be the astronomical figure of 265,000,000 kw or 355,000,000 H.P.—and several times as much in the motor itself. The resultant heat and radiation leakage—even if only a fraction of a per cent.—would volatilize the machine in a few seconds.

These considerations would seem to rule out the possibility of what might be called the "direct" utilization of atomic energy in rocket propulsion, though it will appear later that there is one restricted but very important case where these limitations do not apply.

Some solution must therefore be found employing exhaust velocities well below the thousand km/sec range, though still considerably higher than those obtainable from chemical fuels. Values of 10 km/sec or more would, as we have seen, make interplanetary flight possible without fantastic mass-ratios, and would not introduce the power-dissipation difficulties mentioned above. They would mean, however, that relatively substantial rates of mass-ejection would be demanded, of the order of several tons a second at the take-off of a large spaceship. It would therefore be necessary for the atomic rocket to carry some inert "working fluid" to provide material for the exhaust. This fluid would have to be accelerated and expelled by the nuclear reactor in some manner, presumably by heating and subsequent expansion through a nozzle.

It will be seen that the chief difference between such an atomic rocket and a chemical one is that in the latter case the same material—the fuel—provides both the energy and the working fluid. In the atomic case the two functions are kept distinct. The fuel—if one can now use the expression—would be a relatively small mass of fissile material, which, if it could be avoided, would not be ejected from the rocket at all. The rocket jet—the propellant—might consist of steam, hydrogen or any other gas with suitable characteristics.

This separation of the two duties would remove one of the fundamental limitations imposed on the chemical rocket. Here, the exhaust gases are necessarily the products of chemical reactions chosen primarily for the energy they liberate; but these gases are not those which would give the greatest exhaust velocity after expansion through a nozzle. We have seen in Chapter III that efflux velocity *decreases* as the molecular weight of the gases increases, and that the end-products of the usual reactions have molecular weights between 18 and 44. Elementary gases such as hydrogen and helium have molecular weights of only 2 or 4. The expansion of such gases, under the same conditions of temperature and pressure as the usual combustion products, would therefore, by Equation III.5, yield exhaust velocities *up to four times greater* than those of conventional rockets.

The "secondary" atomic rocket, using nuclear energy to heat a gas of very low molecular weight, thus appears to offer promising possibilities since high exhaust velocities could be obtained at much lower temperatures than with chemical rockets. The performances that might be expected, on purely thermodynamic considerations, are shown by Figure 12 (taken from Shepherd and Cleaver's paper).

These curves are based on Equation III.3, assuming an expansion ratio of 100 and a γ of 1.1, which are believed to be attainable figures for a motor operating in space. For comparison purposes, the exhaust velocity and temperature values for a V.2 motor are shown, though the operating conditions differ considerably (the expansion ratio in particular being much lower).

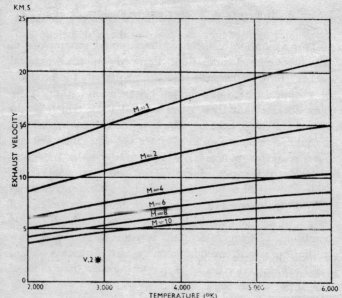

Fig. 12. *Variation of exhaust velocity with molecular weight and chamber temperature (for expansion ratio* 100, $\gamma=1.10$).

The curves show very clearly the great importance of low molecular weights. A motor employing pure hydrogen ($M=2$) at the combustion chamber temperature of V.2 would give a jet speed of over 10 km/sec. If operating temperatures could be increased to considerably higher values —as they certainly will be in the chemical motors of the near future—exhaust speeds approaching the value of 15 km/sec would appear to be in sight.

Hydrogen is by no means the only possible working fluid: it has, unfortunately, very grave disadvantages from the point of view of handling and storage. (Its boiling point is —253° C. and its specific gravity only 0.07). Other materials containing large quantities of hydrogen would be usable, and some of them are listed in the table below.

Table 4

Fluid	Mol. Wt.	Spec. Gravity	B.P. (°C)
Hydrogen, H_2	2.02	0.07	−253
Deuterium, D_2	4.04	0.17	−240
Helium, He	4.00	0.12	−269
Water, H_2O	18.02	1.00	+100
Heavy Water, D_2O	20.04	1.10	+101
Ammonia, HN_3	17.03	0.68	− 33
Methane, CH_4	16.03	0.42	−161

Perhaps the most attractive of these fluids are ammonia and methane. Although their molecular weights, as listed, are quite high, they decompose at sufficiently high temperatures according to the equations

$$CH_4 \rightleftharpoons C + 2\,H_2$$
$$2\,NH_3 \rightleftharpoons N_2 + 3\,H_2$$

The *effective* molecular weights are thus greatly reduced, from 16.03 to 5.34 in the case of methane and from 17.03 to 8.52 in the case of ammonia (which decomposes particularly readily). These values would fall even further at very high temperatures as the hydrogen or nitrogen molecules themselves began to dissociate into free atoms.

It might be mentioned here that this effect, which is a grave disadvantage in the chemical rocket since it represents the reverse of the normal, energy-liberating reaction, is positively advantageous in an atomic rocket, where it may be assumed that ample energy is available from nuclear sources. One could thus have the apparent paradox of a rocket running on water, which is heated atomically to such a high temperature that the reverse reaction

$$2 H_2O = 2 H_2 + O_2$$

is virtually complete. This is of course the precise opposite of what would happen in a chemical rocket burning hydrogen and oxygen.

Practical Considerations

The above discussion has been purely theoretical and though it has shown that nuclear energy can, on paper at least, solve the main problems of interplanetary flight, it now remains to be seen if the practical difficulties can be overcome. One of the most important of these is the problem of heat transfer.

Making certain reasonable assumptions based on present nuclear reactions, it can be shown that the amount of fissile material expended in ejecting a propellant at 10 km/sec is about 10^{-6} of the weight of propellant. Thus only 1 kg (2 pounds) of nuclear fuel would be consumed by a rocket using 1000 tons of working fluid. This sounds a very attractive proposition: but it is necessary to devise some means of transferring enormous quantities of heat from the relatively small amount of active material to the propellant fluid.

The most obvious way of doing this would be by some variant of the uranium reactor or "pile". This, as is well-known, consists of a lattice-work of uranium interspersed with a moderating material (carbon or heavy water) which serves the purpose of slowing down the fast neutrons produced by the fission process. This is necessary to maintain the chain reaction in normal uranium, which is fissioned only by slow-moving ("thermal") neutrons. If the uranium used in the reactor is enriched—i.e. consists largely of the fissile U^{235} isotope—then a so-called "fast neutron reactor" can be built. This does not require any moderating material, and so can be made small enough to stand on a laboratory table—whereas the earlier type of reactor is as large as a house. During the reaction, very large quantities of heat are liberated, and control mechanisms are required to prevent the entire structure from melting down. The excess heat is normally carried out of the system by water or gas circulating through it, and the use of this heat energy to operate some conventional engine is the basis of present attempts to harness nuclear energy for power production. An atomic rocket, based on this principle, is shown schematically in Figure 13 (a).

The first atomic piles, which were water-cooled, operated at temperatures of less than 100 degrees C. If the nuclear rocket is to give substantial improvements in performance over possible chemical motors, Figure 12 shows that it must run at temperatures of 3,000°K, and preferably much higher. This at once introduces very grave difficulties, since uranium metal melts at 1,150°K. Even the use of the oxide would only increase the melting point of the fissile material to about 2,100°K, though other, more refractory compounds, doubtless exist and might be utilized.

The fact that in present-day rockets it is possible to have the chamber walls operating at temperatures far lower (by 1,000°C or more) than the temperature of the burning gases should not give rise to false hopes, since the conditions are totally different. In the chemical rocket the heat energy is actually generated in the reacting gases, and only a part of it leaks back into the surrounding chamber walls.

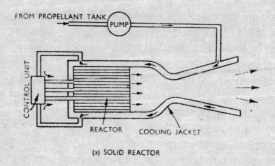

FROM PROPELLANT TANK

PUMP

CONTROL UNIT

REACTOR   COOLING JACKET

(a) SOLID REACTOR

FROM PROPELLANT TANK

PUMP

FROM NUCLEAR

CONTROL UNIT   CONTROL UNIT

"FUEL" TANK

COOLING JACKET

NUCLEAR "FUEL" INJECTORS

(b) GASEOUS REACTOR

Fig. 13. Atomic Rockets (schematic).

The nuclear rocket, however, would generate heat in the solid material of the reactor and transfer it to the originally cold propellant—hence the solid part of the rocket, or some portion of it, must be even hotter than the exhaust gases, since heat energy cannot, as such, flow *up* a thermal gradient.

This argument suggests a second form of atomic rocket in which the heat energy is liberated inside the propellant gas and not transferred to it from elsewhere. In this case the nuclear fuel would be intimately mixed with the working fluid in a reaction chamber and expansion would be allowed to occur. Conditions would thus parallel much more closely those in a conventional rocket and, above all, it would be possible to cool the chamber walls to reasonable temperatures. The schematic diagram of such a "gaseous" system is shown in Figure 13 (b).

Shepherd and Cleaver have discussed the conditions under which this type of motor could operate. It is obviously essential that the quantity of nuclear "fuel" shall be much smaller than the amount of propellant, since this too will be lost by the system. Severe restrictions are also placed on the propellant fluids that can be used, since if they absorb neutrons too readily the reaction will not be self-sustaining. When these factors are all taken into account, it appears that the gaseous reactor is not feasible with known fissile materials. The fundamental difficulty that arises is that the critical radius for such a system (i.e. the minimum size at which the reaction could be self-sustaining) is far too large. For example, a gaseous reactor using hydrogen as a propellant and U^{235} as a fuel, even if it was operating at a pressure of 100 atmospheres, would have to have a chamber radius of 120 metres!

The gaseous reactor, attractive though it is on some grounds, seems therefore an impossibility unless a nuclear reaction with much more favourable critical conditions is discovered.

We are thus forced to return to the solid reactor of Figure 13 (a), and to hope that the engineering difficulties of very high temperature operation can be overcome. There are a number of possibilities in this direction which will certainly be explored, of which perhaps the most promising involve unorthodox methods of heat transfer, and the addition of energy to the exhaust gases during the actual process of expansion.

An additional problem which might also be acute in this type of rocket is that of pumping the propellant through the reactor which, in order to obtain the necessary heat transfer, would have to be sub-divided to give a large surface area. A spaceship at take-off might have to eject propellant at the rate of several tons a second, and if the pressure drop across the reactor became too great the pumping requirements would be prohibitive.

Another objection that is sometimes raised against the use of atomic energy for rocket—or aircraft—propulsion is the danger of lethal radiation (particularly hard gamma rays) from the reactor. This danger is, of course, very real, for a man can be fatally injured even by a practically instantaneous exposure to a high-energy pile. If the rocket was of a long, slender shape, with the crew chamber at one end and the power unit at the other, the amount of shielding material would be relatively small. Moreover, the fuel tanks would themselves provide excellent protection. The shielding weight would however always be substantial and would impose a minimum size below which it would be impracticable to build an atomic rocket. Shepherd[2] has made a quantitative study of the problem and concludes that for a large spaceship the addition of shielding material need not have an appreciable adverse effect on the mass-ratio.

[2] *Journal of the B.I.S.*, **8**, 149-57 (July 1949).

The radiation danger to the crew is however only one of the hazards which must be considered. The power unit of an atomic rocket would always be more or less violently radioactive, even when it had been shut down for a long period, and so precautions would have to be taken to prevent personel approaching it. All servicing would have to be done by robot or remote-control mechanisms of the type developed in the Manhattan Project for handling "hot" materials.

Finally, the exhaust stream of the rocket might itself be radioactive. This would be particularly true if any part of the fissile material was ejected with the propellant, and might make it impossible to use nuclear propulsion anywhere near the Earth's surface owing to the danger of large-scale contamination. In this case it would be necessary to launch the rocket into space by a booster unit using chemical fuels, and the landing would also have to be made with chemical propellants. (This scheme will be discussed further in the next chapter). The atomic drive would thus only be used in space.

Under these conditions, a new possibility is opened up which may be of great importance. Many of the difficulties involved in the design of the atomic rocket are due to the fact that, if we are considering take-offs from the Earth's surface, very large thrusts are necessary—of the order of several thousand tons for a spaceship. However, once the rocket was already travelling in a free orbit round the Earth, the smallest thrusts would be sufficient to produce any required velocity, if the time of application was prolonged accordingly. It would then become feasible to design motors which need produce thrusts only a hundredth or a thousandth of those necessary to lift a rocket away from the Earth, and many constructional problems would be greatly simplified. It might, for example, be possible to employ "pulsed" operation, the motors working for short periods at temperatures and pressures that could not be sustained in steady operation.

One of the most interesting possibilities opened up by such low-thrust rockets, however, is that of utilizing very high exhaust speeds. We have seen (Equation VII.2) that high thrusts and high exhaust speeds cannot be obtained simultaneously owing to excessive power dissipation. This limitation would be removed if low thrusts, and hence accelerations, were employed. The direct use of atomic energy to produce high-speed particles, previously rejected at the beginning of this chapter, would thus appear to enter the picture again; but the difficult problem still remains of organizing the random motions of the sub-atomic fragments into a single direction.

A more promising scheme for the generation and use of very high jet velocities would be what has been christened the "ion rocket". It is easy to produce, by electrostatic fields, beams of ions or electrons travelling at any velocity up to that of light. (This, of course, is the principle of the familiar cathode-ray tube). The thrust developed by such beams is microscopic, although there is a well-known laboratory toy in which a tiny mica paddle-wheel is rolled along a vacuum tube by ion bombardment. But it is conceivable that the same principle might be employed on a relatively large scale for a rocket operating in free space.

Shepherd and Cleaver have investigated the problem mathematically to determine the currents and voltages needed to power an ion rocket. The operating equations show that it is most advantageous to use as ionized material a substance of *high* molecular or atomic weight—the exact reverse of the case for the "thermodynamic" form of nuclear rocket. Assuming mercury ($M = 200.6$) as a propellant, working at an exhaust velocity of 100 km/sec and an acceleration of 0.01 gravities, the device would have to operate at a voltage of about 10,000. Unfortunately the ion currents required would be very high—480 amps per ton of mass accelerated—though the propellant consumption would be only 1 gram per second per ton of mass.

Using higher exhaust velocities would reduce the ion currents by a proportionate amount, but would increase the accelerating voltages and the total power requirements. Electrical energies of the order of thousands of kilowatts would be necessary per ton mass of the rocket, and clearly this scheme is impracticable if conventional generating systems have to be employed.

The possibility still remains that some form of nuclear reaction, emitting charged rather than neutral particles, might be employed as an energy source for such a device: but in the present early (and secret) state of atomic technology this must remain largely a matter of speculation.

*　　　*　　　*　　　*

The above picture of the prospects for the atomic rocket may at first sight appear somewhat depressing in view of the technical problems which arise in all the cases examined. To restore the proper sense of proportion, therefore, it would be well to remember that engineering atomics is in its infancy, and that almost unprecedented technical efforts are being expended upon it in many countries. It is more than probable that quite novel solutions will arise to difficulties which now seem insuperable, and that the schemes described above for employing nuclear energy for propulsion may soon appear as crude as the typical eighteenth century conception of a flying machine.

Even if the atomic rocket does follow closely the patterns outlined above, the whole history of past technical achievement suggests that what now appear fundamental limitations may be surpassed by improved designs and materials. An excellent example of this trend can be found in the development of aviation, where well into the 1920's highly qualified aeronautical engineers could be found explaining that the aeroplane would always be incapable of commercial long-distance operation (i.e. over a thousand miles!) and that its maximum speed would be limited to about 150 m.p.h. These prophecies now seem quite absurd, yet the "absolute limits of performance" which they postulated were shattered, not by radically new inventions which transformed the technical scene, but by a series of steady improvements. None of these (e.g. the retractable undercarriage, variable-pitch airscrews, slots and flaps) was very spectacular in itself, but their combined effect was to improve performance by almost an order of magnitude. The same sequence of events may be expected to occur in the development of the atomic rocket.

Chapter VIII

SPACESHIPS AND SPACE STATIONS

It is not altogether misleading to compare the position of astronautics today with that of heavier-than-air flight in the closing decades of the nineteenth century. Any detailed technical description of the spaceship at the present time might, therefore, be as hopeless a task as predicting, when the Wrights were making their first experiments, the design characteristics of a modern airliner. The situation is further complicated by our present uncertainty about the form that the atomic drive will take when it finally emerges.

Certain conclusions, however, seem inescapable in the light of our earlier discussions. Spaceships for even the most modest missions (e.g. the orbit round the Earth, the circumlunar journey without landing) will have to be largely "expendable", with initial masses scores or hundreds of times their final mass. Much ingenuity has gone into devising constructional techniques which would make this possible. One of the earliest published designs was that evolved by Hermann Oberth while he was technical adviser on the UFA film "Frau Im Mond". (See plate VI). This was a two-step machine, a small upper component being carried into space by a large booster stage fitted with fins. According to Ley, the impressive model which was made from this design was later seized by the Gestapo, and it would be interesting to know its subsequent fate.

A lunar voyage with a two-step rocket would, as we

have seen in Chapter V, be quite out of the question with chemical propellants, and a more radical attempt to get to grips with the problem[1] was made by the Technical Committee of the British Interplanetary Society just before the War. The design evolved was based on the "cellular principle", already mentioned on page 41. The assumption was made (which is now believed to be too optimistic) that *solid* propellants could be developed capable of giving exhaust speeds of well over 4 km/sec. The use of such fuels in self-contained motors was envisaged, so that the problem of pumping and separate storage was eliminated. Against this, however, the "cellules" had to be stressed to withstand the full combustion chamber pressures and temperatures.

Although solid-propellant motors are, of course, uncontrollable once they have been ignited, a certain amount of operating flexibility would be obtained by adjusting the rate and sequence of firing. An automatic ignition system, resembling a small telephone exchange, was designed to fire the tubes in the correct order—an order which could be controlled by a pendulum-operated course-correcting device.

The first five steps would have been used to escape from the Earth and to land on the Moon. The upper step, with the crew container, would hold the fuel for the return journey, and only the crew chamber, weighing about a ton, would finally arrive back on Earth by parachute. The total weight of such a machine, carrying three passengers, was estimated to be about 3,000 tons, a figure which was perhaps very optimistic. (See Plate VII).

[1] *J.B.I.S.*, 5, (Jan. 1939.)

This design was investigated in considerable detail and although it is now largely of historic interest, it did good service in focusing attention on the engineering problems of space flight and was very widely discussed (seriously or otherwise) in the lay and technical press at the time of publication.

More recently[2] a preliminary design study has been made of a composite spaceship using both chemical and atomic propellants. (Plate VIII). In view of the possible dangers of radioactive contamination, it has been assumed that the ship would be taken out of the atmosphere by a large chemically-fuelled booster, burning oxygen and hydrogen. When the booster had been discarded, the atomic drive (using ammonia as propellant) would take over and give orbital velocity to a three-step chemical rocket, which would make the circumnavigation of the Moon and return to an orbit round the Earth, from which the crew would be landed by a much smaller rocket sent up to meet them. The initial weight of the ship would be about 1,200 tons.

The almost insuperable problems involved in designing a ship which can make complete round trips in a single operation suggests more and more forcibly that the orbital-refuelling techniques discussed in the earlier Chapters will play an essential role in astronautics even after an atomic drive becomes available. This in turn suggests that two radically different types of spaceship may evolve, each suited to its particular task and unable to perform any other. The one would be a short-range, powerful rocket whose duty it would be to climb up from the surface of a planet into a circular orbit just outside the atmosphere. This is a

[2] *J.B.I.S.*, **8**, 162-5 (July 1949).

feat which could be performed with the chemical propellants of the near future, if air-resistance braking can be utilized for the return to Earth. The ship envisaged would probably be a two-step rocket, the lower or booster stage falling back by parachute or other aerodynamic means after it had done its work so that it could be used again. The upper step would be winged so that when it re-entered the atmosphere it could land as a glider. (Its empty weight would of course be very low, and its speed would give it world-wide range). This scheme is similar to the German A.9-A.10 project, and still more so to a long-range rocket bomber on which Sanger was working during the War[3].

This "tug" or "ferry" rocket, though it would enter space, would hardly be a true spaceship and would never venture more than a few hundred miles from the surface of the Earth. The deep-space machine, on the other hand, would never enter the atmosphere: it would be assembled in space and would spend all its career circling the planets in free fall, or travelling on the long trajectories cutting the planetary orbits. It would be capable of developing only very small thrusts, so that it could not possibly lift itself against the gravitational field even of a small world like the Moon: but its atomic motors could maintain those thrusts for very prolonged periods.

In normal rocket design we are accustomed to accelerations of several gravities, sustained for a period of a minute or so, but a few "milligee" over a period of one or two days would produce the same final result. This use of relatively low accelerations would enormously simplify the

[3] Information on which has been restricted, until very recently, despite the fact that the British, Americans, French and Russians each possess copies of Sanger's report. One wonders just who was keeping it secret from whom.

construction of the spaceship, since no part need be heavily stressed and the whole structure could be, by terrestrial standards, fantastically flimsy. It would also follow that the ship would be quite unlike the usual present-day conception. Since it need pay no regard to aerodynamics it would have no trace of streamlining. The most obvious shape, indeed, would be a sphere: but this might be ruled out as considerations of atomic shielding demand a long, thin structure with the crew cabin in the "radiation shadow" of the motor. This inevitably suggests a ship consisting of *two* spheres connected by a long cylindrical or lattice structure. The larger sphere would contain the crew, fuel supplies, control mechanisms, etc., while the smaller would house the atomic drive and would be un-approachably radioactive. This "dumb-bell" layout would also provide somewhat improved manoeuvrability as the auxiliary jets used for changing the ship's orientation in space could likewise be in the smaller sphere, at some distance from the centre of mass.

An impression of such a machine in space is given in Plate IX. It is shown here making contact with the "ferry" rocket from Earth, for the purpose of transferring fuel, equipment and personnel. Both machines are in a free orbit at a height of a few hundred miles and would continue to circle together indefinitely until the Earth-based machine used its rockets to cut its speed and so fall back into the atmosphere.

The conception of two rockets, each travelling at 18,000 m.p.h., coming together in this fashion is one that many people find too fantastic to accept. But it must be realised that if the ships are in the same orbit, they are completely at rest with respect to each other. There would be no sense of velocity: indeed, those in the ship would find it difficult not to regard themselves as fixed while the Earth turned beneath them.

In space, travelling on a gravitationally "flat" surface as one would be in these circumstances, it is possible to use very low thrusts and relative accelerations, and there is no *a priori* reason why any required degree of precision or fineness of control should not be achieved, since one could normally take as long as one liked over any manoeuvre. In practice the two ships would probably be brought as near to relative rest as possible within a few kilometres of each other, linked by cable, and slowly drawn together. This is the operation which is depicted in the drawing: it would be supervised by crew-members wearing space-suits (see page 119) and equipped with reaction propulsion devices so that they can move about.

The problem of spaceship manoeuvrability is one of some importance, but it has seldom received any quantitative discussion. There are only two basic ways of altering the attitude or orientation of a body in space—by tangential jets, or by gyroscopes or their equivalent. The rotation produced by jets is permanent: since the body is in a vacuum and no frictional forces are acting, it will retain indefinitely any spin given to it. Jets would therefore be used to neutralise any unwanted rotation: they would hardly be used to change the attitude of a non-rotating ship. Gyroscopes or flywheels would be more suitable for this purpose, since they could move a body's axis from a position of rest in one direction to a position of rest in another.

If one imagines a massive flywheel at the ship's centre of gravity, both bodies being initially at rest, then since the total angular momentum of the system must remain constant, spinning the flywheel in one direction will cause the ship to rotate in the other. This rotation will continue as long as the flywheel is kept spinning, which would require very little power, and it could be stopped at any position by bringing the flywheel to rest again. Since the moment of inertia of the spaceship might be a hundred thousand times that of the largest practicable flywheel, its turning speed would be correspondingly smaller, and in extreme cases it might take several minutes to make a large movement of the ship's axis. In general this would be unimportant, since there would be no particular urgency in such manoeuvres: one would have millions of miles and many days in which to prepare for them.

Many of one's "commonsense" ideas and conceptions are violated in space-flight, and it is particularly difficult for the layman to grasp the fact that there is no connection at all between the direction of motion of a spaceship and the actual orientation of its axis, except during the very brief periods while it is under power or traversing an atmosphere. (As an example of this, one might mention that a V.2 rocket on a high-altitude trajectory is travelling "sideways" during the downward part of its journey, and falls back into the atmosphere very nearly tail-first. It is then quickly swung round by the aerodynamic forces on its fins.)

A spaceship's initial period of powered flight would, of course, be very accurately controlled in direction according to the voyage requirements: there would be no possibility of a major change once the flight velocity had been attained. The only manoeuvres necessary thereafter would be very minor course corrections, which would be made at a later stage in the voyage to allow for the inevitable errors of the initial trajectory, and the final deceleration on approaching the goal. The maximum change of course required should be, at the most, a matter of a few degrees, and to effect this it would be necessary to give the ship a small velocity component approximately at right-angles to its existing velocity vector. (A simple application of the triangle of velocities.) This would be done by turning the ship in the appropriate direction and firing the motors for a few seconds. In the same way the descent into a gravitational field would be carried out by turning the ship towards the planet of destination and reducing the speed of fall by a series of rocket bursts reserved—for reasons of economy—to the last possible moment. This operation, the only feasible way of landing on an airless body such as the Moon, may appear an impossibly dangerous one and, indeed, it is doubtful if it could be carried out by manual control. But it is exactly analogous to what happens when a large liquid-fuel rocket such as V.2 takes off. The machine then rises very slowly under its jet thrust, its stability being maintained by the gyro-control mechanism of the automatic steering device. In the same way, if the thrust was gradually reduced to zero, it could be brought back to rest again on the Earth's surface. This operation would be much simplified by the fact that any planet on which it was necessary would have a much lower gravitational field than the Earth's, and the rate of fall would be correspondingly reduced.

Since the low-thrust, "deep-space" machine described earlier could not make a landing on any body larger than an asteroid or one of the minuter satellites, it would have to carry with it a small auxiliary rocket which would descend to the surface of the planet being investigated. This machine, once it had returned to the parent ship and re-embarked its crew, could be left orbiting the planet for the benefit of future expeditions.

As has been remarked before, the whole design of spaceships would be enormously simplified as soon as it becomes possible to refuel at the end of a journey, instead of having to carry fuel for the complete round trip. Indeed, the first objective of any extra-terrestrial colony, once the problem of sheer physical survival had been overcome, would be to locate and refine the materials necessary for rocket fuel manufacture. The atomic rocket, which might eventually be able to operate on such a simple and common substance as water, might then be at a still more overwhelming advantage over the chemical rocket with its complex and often exotic propellants. In particular, if fuel supplies can be obtained from the Moon—and presumably our satellite is made of much the same materials as this planet—it would then become economical to use this source to refuel orbiting spaceships leaving the Earth. The quarter-million mile shipment from the Moon would actually require less energy than the few-hundred-mile climb through the atmosphere.

Looking somewhat further afield, the fact that the atmospheres of the giant planets and at least one of their satellites (Titan, largest moon of Saturn) seem mainly composed of ammonia and methane, two of the best propellants for atomic rockets, is certainly a stimulating thought.

It will take generations, perhaps centuries, to develop all these variations of technique: but by successive improvements of design, and by exploiting the slowly uncovered and, today, unguessed-at resources of the planets, spaceflight will evolve from a fabulous scientific feat into an everyday enterprise which will be taken completely for granted by the scattered civilizations whose lives will depend upon it. The development of commercial aviation—the wildest of fantasies a life-time ago—will perhaps be paralleled in many respects by the history of astronautics. We now accept, almost without thought or question, speeds, ranges and powers which even a generation ago would have been dismissed as impossible. It is salutory to ask what the Edwardians—let alone the Victorians—would have thought of a vehicle which required 25,000 h.p. and 50 tons of fuel to carry no more than a hundred passengers on a single journey. [4] Technically, the modern airliner is probably half-way between the steam locomotive and the spaceship— and it is much nearer the latter in time.

In the next chapter we will discuss some of the many subsidiary problems which will have to be solved before spaceships can be built, but before leaving the subject for the present it may be as well to deal with a point which, sooner or later, everyone interested in astronautics asks himself—must it be assumed that spaceships will necessarily be rocket-propelled? May not the rocket, in fact, play the same rôle in the conquest of space that the balloon played in the conquest of the air?

This *cri-de-coeur* is not uncommon among those who have practical dealings with rocketry, and there have been many proposals or suggestions of other devices which might be used in interplanetary flight. Now that we are breaking into the secret treasure-house of the atomic nucleus, perhaps we may at last uncover forces which will teach us something about that most elusive yet universal of all phenomena, gravity. It is true that the short-range forces

[4] The Bristol Brabazon I.

which hold the nucleus together (or not, as the case may be) appear to be non-gravitational; but they are certainly immensely powerful and even if they are not related to gravity, they may yet provide us with new ways of overcoming it.

However, even if we possessed some means of affecting or neutralizing gravity, the fact must not be forgotten that a perfectly definite amount of work, calculated according to the principles laid down in Chapter II, has to be done in conveying a body on the Earth to any other planet. That work must come from somewhere. It does not matter in the least what the mode of propulsion may be: some forms might be more efficient than others, but all would require *at least* this minimum amount of energy, which must be provided by the fuel stores of the ship. Thus an electrically-operated anti-gravity device, which had to be energised by conventional generating equipment burning chemical fuels, would be quite useless. The weight of the intermediate turbines and generators would make the apparatus far heavier and far less efficient than a rocket burning the same fuel directly. The position might, however, be different if an atomically-powered generator was used.

Such conceptions as "gravitational screens" (as used in Wells' famous novel, "The First Men In The Moon") must be ruled out for similar reasons. Wells' "Cavorite", indeed, flatly violated the law of the conservation of energy.

On 10th February, 1859, Michael Faraday wrote in his journal: "Who knows what is possible when dealing with gravity?" Ninety years later, we are still asking that same question, but with far greater prospects of obtaining a reply. That we will get it before we conquer space the hard way, using the rocket with all its limitations, is unlikely. One day the rocket, like all things, will be superseded; but its successor will be the creation of technologies as yet unborn.

The Space Station

From the conception of spaceships circling a planet for reconnaissance or refuelling, it was a natural step to consider the possibility of permanent orbital structures—"space stations"—and although this subject is perhaps subsidiary to the main theme of astronautics, it opens up so many important and stimulating prospects that it merits careful study.

The idea of space stations was originated, like a good many other things, by Oberth, but was developed in great detail by two Austrian engineers, Captain Potočnik and Count von Pirquet. As first conceived, the space station was regarded largely as a refuelling depot for spaceships on their way to the planets, but it was soon realized that it would perform many other valuable functions.

In the first place, it would provide the ideal site for an astronomical or meteorological observatory. The wonderful photographs of the Earth taken from V.2 rockets show what a wealth of detail is visible from space: the weather situation over half the globe could be seen literally at a glance, and could be continually televised to ground stations. As an orbital base a few hundred miles from the Earth would complete a revolution every ninety minutes, a considerable part of the planet could be kept under almost continuous observation. A station a few thousand miles up would observe practically the whole Earth: this could also be done economically by a station just outside the atmosphere but with its orbit passing over the Poles: it would obtain a close-up of every part of the planet once every twelve hours, at the most.

It need hardly be pointed out that these facts have political and military implications almost as great as their scientific ones. Probably the interest expressed by the United States government in the subject of satellite bases is inspired by these. It would not, of course, be necessary to have a *manned* station to carry out such observations, and the first steps in this direction will involve sending automatic, television-equipped missiles into free orbits round the Earth.

As an astronomical observatory, the space-station opens up dazzling prospects. The Earth's atmosphere, as is well-known, is a severe handicap to astronomical research. Not only do its lack of homogeneity and constant minute tremors reduce telescopic definition and set an upper limit to the magnification that can be employed with even the largest instruments, but it is also virtually opaque to wide—and extremely important—bands of the spectrum in the ultra-violet and infra-red. This state of affairs has reduced astronomers to the position of colour-blind men groping in a fog; and when one considers what they have already learned under these conditions, it is obvious that entry into space will revolutionize their science. This revolution has, indeed, already started with high-altitude V.2 ascents.

In physics, also, there is a vast range of experiments which can only be carried out with great difficulty, if at all, at the surface of the Earth. Large-scale vacuum research is a case in point: it is obviously impossible to conduct experiments demanding very large mean-free-paths in terrestrial laboratories.

Even more interesting possibilities are opened up by the fact that the space-station, like all freely moving bodies, no matter how near the Earth they may be (see p. 114) would be under conditions of zero gravity. This is a state of affairs that has never been reproduced, except momentarily, at the Earth's surface. Its effect on chemical reactions and physical or biological processes is unknown and such studies may result in very important discoveries.

Elaborate plans for the space station were drawn up by Captain Potočnik, who published them in a book "Das Problem der Befahrung des Weltraums", under the pseudonym "Hermann Noordung". He envisaged three structures floating in space near each other and connected by cables. The main unit would have been built around a very large parabolic mirror which would act as the collector for a solar motor providing power for the station.

A more modern conception of the space-station, built in a single self-contained unit, was recently published by H. E. Ross.[5] The main part of the structure is a parabolic annular mirror about 70 metres (200 feet) in diameter, with a system of pipes carrying water or some other fluid at its focus. This mirror would intercept nearly 4,000 kW. (5,500 h.p.) of energy when pointed towards the Sun, and after conversion losses at least a quarter of this should become available as electrical power. (It may be pointed out that a heat engine would be working under almost ideal conditions in space, since the low-temperature part of the system could be in shadow, where the temperature approaches absolute zero.)

[5] *J.B.I.S.*, **8**, 1-19, Jan. 1949.

Plate XII

TYPICAL LUNAR LANDSCAPE (MARE IMBRIUM).

Plate XIII

From the painting by Frank Tinsley

BUILDING THE LUNAR BASE

Construction crews at work in space-suits and pressurized tractor vehicles.

Behind the mirror would be the living quarters and laboratories, arranged symmetrically around the axis of the station. (Plate X).

Since the physiological effects of weightlessness are unknown, it seems desirable to provide what may be loosely termed "artificial gravity", and this can be readily done by rotating the station slowly about its axis. The outward centrifugal force thus generated would be quite indistinguishable from gravity and would have a value of 1g if the station turned once every seven seconds. Probably a lower value would be chosen, to reduce structural stresses. There would, of course, be zero "gravity" at the axis of the station and it would increase linearly towards the rim. At all points on the station, "up" would be towards the central axis: men on opposite sides of the structure would be standing with their heads pointed towards each other.

Once the station had been set turning, its axial spin would be retained indefinitely, and the only evidence of its existence would be the apparent gravity and the fact that the stars were moving. It would clearly be extremely undesirable, and wasteful of power, to stop the rotation if personnel or stores had to be brought aboard, and one way of getting over this would be to approach the station along its central axis where "gravity" was zero. An alternative method which Ross proposes in his design is the use of a separately movable arm (the lattice-tower behind the mirror in Plate XI). This would normally remain at rest in space while the mirror and the remainder of the station rotated in front of it. At the end nearer the axis it would have a chamber fitted with airlocks—one opening into space, the other capable of coupling with a similar lock in the station.

Visitors from an approaching rocket, once their ship had come to rest a kilometre or so away, would cross the intervening space by means of a small reaction device or a cable link and enter the chamber. The lattice arm would then be set rotating until it was synchronized with the station, when the airlocks would be coupled together and the visitors could enter.

The fact that the station was rotating would naturally make astronomical observation somewhat difficult, but this is a problem which astronomers on the Earth have also had to contend with—though their instruments have only to neutralize one rotation every 24 hours instead of one every 7 seconds. However, the principles involved are the same and a device known as a "coelostat" is capable of giving a stationary view of the revolving heavens. This would be fitted to the large telescopes seen projecting along the axis of the station.

Ross has worked out in some detail the provisioning of such a large space station, assuming a staff of 24, and it appears that the total food, air and water supplies for a year would be of the order of 70 tons, which is a not excessive figure. This assumes some reclamation of used materials and interesting problems in air-conditioning are obviously involved, but these do not demand anything essentially new. Conditions not dissimilar to those in a space station have had to be faced in high-altitude aircraft and, even more so, in submarines.

Presumably, with the development of astronautics, space stations will be constructed at varying distances from the Earth (and not all, necessarily, in circular orbits) to carry out numerous different duties. The most important of these will, of course, be the maintenance and refuelling of spaceships, and perhaps their navigational control as they approach or leave the Earth. Stations with other, more specialized functions will be built as occasion demands: one of these—the television relay station—was described in a proposal made by the author some years ago. [6]

It is well-known that the very-high-frequency waves employed by television and similar services handling large quantities of information (*e.g.*, "Ultrafax", certain radar navigational devices, etc.) are limited in range by the curvature of the Earth. To overcome this, chains of repeater stations have had to be built at intervals of about fifty miles, or exceedingly expensive coaxial cables (costing some £1,000 a mile) have to be laid. Even by these methods programmes can be carried only from one small region to another: the provision of television services over the whole of a large area by means of a network of repeaters would be hopelessly uneconomic, except where population densities were very high. Even the provision of airborne relay stations is a palliative, not a cure, and the problem of trans-oceanic television seems insuperable.

A single space station, on the other hand, could provide television coverage to almost half the Earth, since every point on the hemisphere below would be visible from it. This would make available the use of centimetre waves, with their enormous traffic-handling capacity. The power needed to give a good service over the hemisphere is very low—comparable to that of a single station such as the B.B.C.'s Alexandra Palace transmitter.

Three stations, 120° apart in an orbit above the equator, could provide complete coverage over all the Earth. They

* *Wireless World*, **51**, 305-8, Oct. 1945.

could be linked to each other by microwave beams and so, using two repeaters at the most, programmes could be relayed from any one point on the globe to any other point, or any form of broadcast service could be provided.

It would, of course, be inconvenient if the space station relays were moving quickly across the sky, as would be the case were they in orbits near the Earth's surface. (A satellite 500 miles up would pass from horizon to horizon in about 15 minutes.) However, if the relays were in the so-called 24-hour orbit, 36,000 kms (22,000 miles) above the surface, they would make one revolution in the same time as the Earth itself turned on its axis and *so would appear immovably fixed in the sky*. Unlike all other celestial objects they would neither rise nor set: receiving aerials on the Earth, once aimed at them, could then be left locked in position. Although there would be some tendency for the stations to drift slightly round their orbits owing to the perturbations of the Sun and Moon, this could be corrected by occasional ejections of mass in the appropriate direction.

This chain of satellite stations could not only solve the otherwise apparently intractable problem of world-wide television, but, perhaps more important and of far greater economic importance, it could eventually replace the thousands of radio and telegraph stations, and the millions of miles of cable, which now comprise our planet's communication system. It could also provide many services which are now impossible and would greatly improve existing ones which rely on the uncertainties of ionospheric reflection: moreover it would be almost immune from the electrical disturbances which occasionally disrupt terrestrial networks.

The orbital relay may begin to change the pattern of

world communications within a few decades, for much could be done with large, unmanned rockets as an intermediate solution even before the true space station becomes possible. Here, perhaps, will be the first major impact of astronautics upon commerce as opposed to science; but it will not be the last.

Several other orbits of peculiar interest also exist and may possibly be occupied by space stations in the course of time. There is, for example, a point on the line between Earth and Moon, and 58,000 kms (36,000 miles) from the Moon, at which a body would always remain between the two worlds, moving so that it kept on their line of centres. [7]

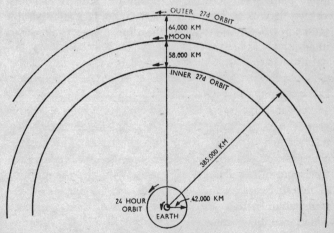

Fig. 14. "Stationary" orbits round the Earth.

[7] A. C. Clarke, "Stationary Orbits", *Journal of the British Astronomical Association,* 57, 232-7, Dec. 1947. These orbits would not be naturally stable: they represent degenerate solutions of the 3-body problem.

(This, it should be mentioned, is nothing to do with the "neutral-point", which is in quite a different place.) Still more surprising, there is a similar orbit 64,000 kms (40,000 miles) *beyond* the Moon, at which the same phenomenon would happen. A body here would always be invisible from the Earth, being permanently eclipsed by the Moon. As it would appear fixed over the very centre of our satellite's hidden hemisphere, it would be an ideal site for a radio transmitter when the far side of the Moon is colonized.

All these orbits are shown in Figure 14, which is drawn to scale. Since similar positions exist with respect to the other planets—in addition to the infinity of more orthodox orbits—it will be seen that there is no lack of desirable sites for space stations when the time comes to construct them.

Chapter IX

SUBSIDIARY PROBLEMS

In this chapter we hope to tidy-up some of the more important loose-ends that may have worried the reader, and to discuss the solutions of certain difficulties which, though subsidiary to the main problems of power and energy, will have to be dealt with before interplanetary flight becomes possible. Not all of these can be foreseen today, any more than all the problems of aeronautics could have been envisaged when the first men took to the air, but there is no reason to suppose that the ingenuity and skill which have provided all the intricate devices making the modern airliner possible will fail us when the conquest of space begins.

The Physiology of Space Flight

Astronautics is unique in the number of sciences which must contribute to its consummation: they range from mathematics to medicine, from physics to physiology. Some of the most interesting, and perhaps most difficult, problems of space flight may well be the medical ones. No human being has ever experienced, save in a few seconds of free fall, the sensation of weightlessness, and it is possible that this may have harmful effects if maintained over prolonged periods of time.

It is not always realized why weightlessness is the normal

condition in space, irrespective of one's distance from gravitating bodies. It would be experienced both on a space station just outside the Earth's atmosphere (where "g" has practically the same value as at the surface) or in a spaceship far beyond Pluto.

We only experience the force known as weight when we resist the efforts of gravity to make us fall towards the centre of the Earth. A man in a stationary lift feels normal weight, but as soon as the cable breaks he becomes instantly "weightless". In a spaceship or a space station *moving in a free orbit* the condition would be the same as in the falling lift: only when acceleration was applied by using the rocket motors would the sensation of weight return—and this, of course, only occurs for a few minutes during a voyage which may last for months.

All the normal bodily functions can still operate in the apparent absence of gravity: many, indeed, can still work under the far more rigorous conditions of *inverted* gravity. But the balance-organs—the semi-circular channels of the inner ear, which act as our spirit-levels—would be useless under free-fall conditions and the conflicting messages they would send to the brain might produce serious disturbances, quite possibly a nausea even more incapacitating than air-sickness. This might be overcome by training, or by suitable drugs, but if these remedies were ineffective it would be necessary to produce a pseudo-gravity by rotating the spaceship on its axis, as described in the previous chapter. The rate of rotation required is comparatively slow: in the pre-war B.I.S. ship (page 94) one revolution every three seconds would have given normal gravity at the walls.

If, on the other hand, one can become "acclimatized" to

weightlessness, life in a spaceship would resemble the levitation dream which most people have experienced at one time or another. Objects placed in the air would stay there until an air current disturbed them: there would be no up or down or indeed any preferential direction, and the touch of a finger would set one drifting from wall to wall. It is sometimes forgotten, however, that even if weight vanished, inertia would be unaffected, and it would be dangerous to ignore this fact. An inexperienced astronaut who jumped the width of a large room would be ill-advised, despite the deceptive slowness with which the opposite wall approached, to underestimate the impact and use his hands to check his leisurely fall. He might easily break his wrists if he did.

Living on the other planets will necessarily mean growing accustomed to varying gravitational fields, but this is a different matter from the complete absence of gravity. It is a fortunate fact that all the other bodies in the Solar System on which landings are possible have lower surface gravities than Earth's, and men would accordingly be at a muscular advantage on them. The only drawback of this would be that on their return to their own world it might be some time before they grew accustomed to their "abnormal" heaviness: they would also have acquired a contempt for heights which might have unfortunate results.

A common impression exists that space-flight would require excessively high initial accelerations, there being an almost universal belief among laymen that a rocket would be "fired-off" nearly as violently as an artillery shell. This, of course, is completely incorrect, and we have seen that even unmanned missiles such as V.2 and "Viking" do not employ very high accelerations. In any case, there is no reason why accelerations of 5 or even 10 g should not be used if the rocket can be stressed to withstand them. The limitation here is mechanical rather than physiological. Men in good health can stand surprisingly high accelerations if they are properly positioned. In a series of tests during the War, the Germans found that even in the "sitting upright" position men could tolerate 7.5 g without loss of consciousness (though with "blackout") and 10 to 12 g for periods of up to 3 minutes in the horizontal position without disturbance. At 10 g one would reach circular velocity in $1\frac{1}{2}$ minutes.

This matter is of some importance in view of the necessity of reducing "gravitational loss" by short firing times as discussed in Chapter IV. Of course, the crew would be incapable of much physical action during a 5 or 10 g take-off, but this is immaterial as the rocket's ascent would certainly be automatically controlled.

The task of providing air, food and water in space is one which can be solved in principle even now: it might be stated that the requirements are not excessive (see page 108) and it is very likely that one's calorie intake would be much reduced under low or zero gravity. The necessary oxygen to replenish the air would be carried in the liquid state, or perhaps as hydrogen peroxide, which can provide in compact form water, oxygen and heat. Some ingenuity has been expended in devising air-conditioning plants for spaceships, a favourite proposal being that the excess carbon dioxide should be removed by freezing, simply by circulating the used air on the cold, shadowed side of the ship.

The question of temperature control in space is one concerning which there are many misconceptions. A very common idea exists that "space is cold" whereas, of course, space can have no temperature at all: only a material body can possess this. Near the Earth's orbit, about 1.4 kilowatts (1.9 h.p.) of solar radiation are intercepted by every square metre facing the Sun, and if much of this was absorbed by a body in space it would become rather hot—in extreme cases, its sunlit parts might reach temperatures of 100° C. The exact temperature distribution throughout the body would depend on its conductivity and reflecting power: silvered or brightly painted objects would absorb little radiation and would remain quite cold even in full sunlight. (Some actual figures for simplified cases are given in Appendix IX.) It would be easy, therefore, to maintain the temperature of the spaceship at a comfortable level, at least for journeys in the region between Venus and Mars, where the solar radiation intensity varies from twice to half its value near the Earth. It must not be forgotten, moreover, that a considerable amount of heat would be generated by the crew's bodies and the ship's auxiliary mechanisms, so that the problem would often be that of discarding excess heat rather than the reverse.

Cosmic Rays

Interplanetary space, though practically empty of matter, is continuously traversed by radiations of which the visible light from the Sun, stars and planets forms only a small portion. Most of these radiations would be stopped completely by even the thinnest sheet of metal, but the most penetrating of all—the so-called "cosmic rays"—would pass through a spaceship almost as easily as sunlight through glass. It has often been suggested that this radiation might be dangerous, or even fatal, to space-travellers.

Our knowledge of cosmic rays is now in a state of flux and will be greatly expanded in the next few years as a result of high-altitude rocket research. It appears, however, that charged particles (perhaps protons) of enormous energy arrive at the Earth from all directions and penetrate into the atmosphere, producing an extremely complex series of secondary radiations—gamma-rays, mesons and other atomic debris—on their way towards the surface. The radiations observed at sea level consist of these "secondaries", together with any of the original "primaries" that have survived their passage through the atmosphere.

As one leaves the Earth's surface, the total intensity of radiation increases rapidly with height to a peak at about 20 kilometres (12 miles) where the value may be 50 or more times that at sea level, the actual figures varying in a complicated manner with latitude and other factors. At still greater heights, the total intensity falls again as there is no longer enough air for the production of "secondaries" in such large quantities. Out in space only the primary rays are present and the general level of intensity is perhaps 15 times that at the surface.

There can be no question of shielding a spaceship completely against cosmic rays, for it would require about a metre of lead to produce the same screening effect as the Earth's atmosphere. Thin shields might actually *increase* the amount of radiation by providing a source of secondary rays, many of which would in any case be produced in the walls of the spaceship by the impact of the primaries.

The cosmic rays that are blasting through our bodies every second of our lives do not seem to do us any harm, and in very-high-altitude flights men have spent several hours at levels where the intensity is much greater than it is out in free space. Moreover, some races (such as the Andes Indians) have spent their entire lives at altitudes where the intensity is considerably greater than at sea-level. It would appear, therefore, that cosmic rays do not present any danger to astronautics—except, possibly, in regions of space where the radiation level might be abnormally high owing, for example, to the focusing effect of magnetic fields. If such regions do exist they could easily be detected and avoided.

It is also possible—indeed very probable—that there are extensive electrostatic fields between the planets, resulting in potential differences of billions of volts. When a spaceship approached a planet there would therefore be a considerable charge to dissipate, but it would be neutralized in the outer layers of the atmosphere or through the highly-conducting exhaust itself. In any case it could not be a danger to the occupants of the ship, as they would be electrostatically shielded by the metal walls.

The Spacesuit

For the exploration of airless bodies like the Moon, or for such operations as orbital refuelling or assembling structures in space, it would be necessary to design what have been christened "spacesuits" so that men can exist and work under considerable extremes of temperature and in a vacuum. Such suits would have much in common with a modern self-contained diving-dress but would have to meet more stringent requirements. They would carry enough oxygen for several hours, and would be fitted with short-range radio sets so that their occupants could talk to each other and to the parent ship. If they were required only for use in space, they might consist simply of cylinders with flexible tubes and gauntlets for the occupants' arms, and large transparent "bubbles" at the same end for vision: no movable legs would be necessary and this would much simplify design. For work on a planet or satellite with appreciable gravity, legs would obviously be required, and some ingenuity would be needed to prevent the internal air-pressure from making the suit rigid so that the unfortunate occupant did not become spread-eagled, unable to bend his limbs. When its evolution is complete, the spacesuit may well be almost as complicated as the spaceship, of which indeed it will be a microcosm.

Meteors

The possible danger to spaceships from meteors is one of the objections which critics of space flight have raised on innumerable occasions, and is a subject on which widely varying and contradictory statements have been made. On the one hand it has been suggested that a rocket would be riddled by cosmic debris as soon as it left the atmosphere: on the other, it has been asserted that the danger from meteoric bombardment is so small as to be unworthy of notice. It seems probable that, as is usually the case, the truth lies between these extremes: but until recently no quantitative estimates were available.

A detailed study of this important question has been

made by G. Grimminger in connection with the U.S. Air Force's PROJECT RAND, and his conclusions have now been published in an unclassified report.[1] The fundamental fact in the problem is the number of meteors of all sizes hitting the Earth every 24 hours, and this has been calculated by extrapolation from visual observations. The results (due to Watson) can be no more than first approximations and may require revision in the light of more recent radar observations. The table below (a shortened version of that in Grimminger's paper) gives the sizes, masses and numbers of meteors in every magnitude, per 24 hours. A 6th magnitude meteor would be barely visible to the naked eye on a very dark night, while one of magnitude —3 would be comparable to Venus at her brightest.

Table 5

Visual magnitude	No. per magnitude	Mass (gm.)	Diameter (cm.)
−3	28,000	4	1.3
0	450,000	0.25	0.5
3	7×10^6	0.016	0.2
6	110×10^6	0.001	0.08
9	18×10^8	0.00006	0.03
15	45×10^{10}	2.5×10^{-7}	0.005
30	45×10^{16}	2.5×10^{-13}	0.00005

It will be seen that meteors over 1 cm. in diameter are negligibly rare when compared with those of smaller sizes—

[1] RAOP 18, which has been printed in the *Journal of Applied Physics*, October 1948.

the numbers of which are truly enormous, far higher than the few score millions a day sometimes gleefully quoted by critics of space flight. But these figures—taken over the whole area of the Earth—mean nothing until related to the area of the spaceship and the toughness of its walls.

Grimminger has derived curves showing what thicknesses of dural and steel will be penetrated by meteors of the various magnitudes. For a dural hull of the thickness employed in normal aircraft construction (0.02-0.05 inches) stony meteors down to magnitude 14 might penetrate, while the rarer iron meteors could be dangerous down to magnitude 16. For a steel hull of the same thickness, the limiting magnitudes are 11 and 13 for the two types of meteors. This means that in the most unfavourable cases meteors only a few thousandth of an inch across might cause damage.

Statistical theory is then employed to derive some extremely interesting tables (too long to be reproduced here) for the case of a body 300 miles from the Earth's surface and with a plan area of 1,000 square feet, about five times that of V.2. The tables give the numbers of hits per hour for meteors of any magnitude, and the "waiting times" for 1:1, 100:1 and 1,000:1 chances of *not* being hit. To quote some results, a rocket of the above size with a dural hull .04 inches thick would run about 1 chance in 30 of being penetrated on the 100 hour lunar trip. This is an appreciable risk, but a slightly thicker skin would very greatly reduce it: for one-eight inch steel the risk would be less than 1 in 10,000 on the lunar voyage. Moreover, it must be realized that the minute puncture caused by these "limiting size" meteors—far smaller than grains of sand—would in the vast majority of cases do no damage at

Plate XIV   *From the painting by R.A. Smith*

SATURN
As seen from a distance of 230,000 miles. Dione in foreground.

Plate XV   *From the painting by R. A. Smith*

MARS

*As seen from a distance of 15,000 miles above Sinus Sabaeus. Deimos in
foreground, Phobos transiting planet.*

all, but would merely add to the leakage inevitable in any pressurized structure.

It has also been pointed out (by Whipple) that a very thin sheet of metal an inch from the outer wall of the spaceship would act as a sort of "meteor bumper", against which the meteor would vaporize itself—and some of the "bumper"—without any damage to the actual wall of the ship.

It seems, therefore, in the light of our present knowledge, that it is probably not worth while taking any special precautions against meteors for relatively short voyages such as the journey to the Moon. For space stations or interplanetary rockets, meteors may represent a real danger (particularly at the times of the great periodic showers) but it is one that can be very greatly reduced by fairly simple means.

It has sometimes been suggested, often by people who should have known better, that meteors would be a menace to lunar explorers. A brief calculation will show that, assuming the meteor frequency at the Moon's surface to be the same as in space, an object as small as a man has a negligible chance of being hit. Moreover, it now seems highly probable that meteors are very rare indeed on the Moon: their impact (which in the case of the larger ones should be easily visible from the Earth) has never been observed except perhaps in one or two cases. This suggests that the Moon has an extremely tenuous atmosphere which, because of the low gravity, would be much deeper than the Earth's and hence a much more effective meteor shield. The detection of such an atmosphere (density 10^{-4} of the Earth's at sea-level) has in fact recently been reported. [2]

[2] Y. N. Lipski: *Proceedings of the Academy of Science, U.S.S.R.* **65** 465-468 (April 1949).

Meteors, it should be noted, are stopped in the Earth's atmosphere at a height where the density is less than this by a factor of about 100.

Navigation in Space

The navigator of a spaceship has one considerable advantage over his counterpart in terrestrial forms of transport. He can always, except during the rare intervals when it might be hidden by the Sun, see his destination; and the framework of stars is always visible around him to give a perfect, unchanging reference system. Moving against that background of stars, with their positions known to an incredible degree of accuracy, are the various planets: it would only be necessary to observe the angles between them and the Sun to determine the location of the spaceship.

Once his position *and velocity* had been accurately determined—which would be done as soon as possible after leaving Earth—the navigator could calculate his future position at any time, since nothing could alter the predetermined path of the ship, save the firing of the motors or the approach to another planet. This type of calculation is, of course, exactly what an astronomer does to determine the orbit of a comet, but at present it requires a great many man-hours of work. In future it will no doubt be done in a few minutes or seconds by specialised calculating apparatus of the type now being developed on a very large scale: it is quite possible that the spaceship would merely take the observations while the "fix" and the resulting orbit would be calculated by ground stations with which it was in radio contact. In this way much more elaborate and powerful computing equipment could be used than could ever be carried in a spaceship. (Even the observations might be done from Earth, as the ship could easily be followed in large telescopes during its initial few days of flight.)

It is also possible that radio position-fixing methods might be used in certain cases, particularly in the vicinity of the Earth. A transmitter on Earth with a "slave" on the Moon could produce a set of position-lines filling an enormous volume of space, and suitable phasing circuits could keep it from rotating despite the movement of the Moon in its orbit.

Radar cannot be used over astronomical distances, unless very large ground stations are employed, but it might be extremely valuable as a short-range aid in making the approach to an airless world such as the Moon, where the altitude had to be known very precisely in order to carry out the landing manoeuvres. This information would probably be fed directly to the automatic mechanism controlling the descent.

Communiciaton [3]

It is obvious that good communications systems will be even more important in space flight than in aviation. Until quite recently the idea of sending radio messages over interplanetary distances seemed to many people almost as fantastic as space travel itself, but in January, 1946, the United States Signal Corps performed the far more

[3] Most of the material in this section is condensed from the author's paper, "Electronics and Space-flight", in the March 1948 *Journal of the British Interplanetary Society*.

difficult feat of obtaining a radio-echo from the Moon. Even before this demonstration, it was known that existing equipment was quite capable of signalling over distances of many millions of miles.

Three main types of communication circuit may be expected to arise in practice: (1) planet to ship; (2) planet to planet; and (3) ship to ship. The last two categories lie in the more remote future, but the first, if it is taken to include the control and telemetering of missiles beyond the atmosphere, is already of practical importance.

It is obvious that the equipment which a spaceship can carry is strictly limited in weight and dimensions, whereas the corresponding equipment on Earth can be as large and powerful as desired. There are certain restrictions, however, on the frequencies which can be employed by a station operating on the Earth. As is well known, the ionosphere or Heaviside Layer reflects back to the surface all radio waves of low frequency, and hence these cannot be employed for interplanetary communication. This loss, fortunately, is of no importance as such relatively long waves (30 metres or more) cannot be readily beamed and so their employment would never be considered.

The next eight octaves of the spectrum—the short-wave radio band, the centimetre and millimetre waves, the infra-red and visible light waves, down to the near ultra-violet—are all available for communication purposes, though some millimetre and infra-red regions suffer from heavy atmospheric absorption. This gives a "window" to space wide enough to pass a range of frequencies about a thousand million times as great as that on the familiar medium-wave bands of our domestic radio sets!

The centimetre waves, which can now be generated very high power levels and can be beamed with as much accuracy as light, appear to be ideal for most astronautical purposes. As our techniques improve, the millimetre and infra-red regions will become available, but modulated-light or "photophone" systems have already reached a high state of development and could be used in the near future for communication over astronomical distances. Though clouds and haze limit their use on the Earth, their extreme simplicity would make them very suitable for ship-to-ship contacts in space.

Whatever purpose electromagnetic waves are used for, certain requirements have to be fulfilled. We need a means of generating the waves at a sufficiently high power level, and then of modulating them by speech, vision or in any other manner required. In the radio range the generator would be some type of vacuum tube, probably a magnetron: in the optical range it might be a gas-discharge tube, some types of which can produce thousand million candle-power flashes.

The waves must next be beamed from a radiating device such as a parabolic reflector or a metal lens—and this at once introduces considerable complications. To save power we will be forced to use narrow beams, and these must therefore be aimed accurately and kept in position despite all movements of the bodies concerned. If one of them is a space rocket, this may mean gyro-stabilised arrays like those which battleships use to keep their radar aerials steady despite pitching and rolling. However, stabilisation of the entire ship would be preferable, and much simpler, unless made impossible by the need for artificial gravity. Fortunately, various ways are now known whereby a radio

array can be kept automatically beamed at ("locked on") a moving object.

The powers needed for any type of communication service over any distance can be easily calculated (see Appendix, Equation IX.3) and tables can be drawn up for various distances, sizes of aerial system, etc. On the conservative assumption that 1 square metre is a practical size for a spaceship's array, while 100 square metres would be a reasonable size for a fixed ground station, we find that at a wavelength of 10 cm. (frequency 3,000 Mc/sec.) we could *with present-day types of equipment* transmit speech to a spaceship more than 10,000,000 kms. away, or send morse to a ship well beyond the orbit of Mars. Two planet-based systems each with 100 square metre arrays could communicate by morse between Earth and Saturn!

Even these figures are only an indication of what could be done with sufficient effort. Physically, a 100 square metre array might be a metal parabola about 40 feet in diameter. At Manchester University one 200 feet across has been built for astronomical research!

One very important use of radio in space will be for "homing" purposes. Despite the perpetually perfect visibility, an orbital fuel cache or even a space-station would not always be easy to find telescopically from a great distance. A very small radio beacon, however, if broadcasting a continuous-wave signal at a power level of a fraction of a watt, could be picked up thousands or even millions of kilometres away, particularly if special "narrow-band" techniques were used.

It can be said, therefore, that even today interplanetary communication circuits would present no great technical difficulties. There is one limitation to such circuits, however, that will never be overcome, for it is set by the finite speed of radio waves. It takes 1.3 seconds for a signal to reach the Moon, so there would always be an annoying time lag of over $2\frac{1}{2}$ seconds if one attempted to carry on a conversation with anyone at this distance. In the cases of the planets the time lags would be much greater, and a continuous two-way conversation would be impossible. It would take five minutes to get a reply from Venus at her nearest, and about nine minutes in the case of Mars: the times for the outer planets would be several hours.

It has often been suggested that a spaceship could be equipped with radar to detect meteors, presumably so that evasive action could be taken. This idea can easily be shown to be quite impracticable, altogether apart from the impossibility of rapid manoeuvres in a spaceship. As Table 5 shows, a meteor even 1 cm. across is incredibly rare, and a rather large spaceship might expect to be hit by one every quarter of a million years! But even such a giant among meteors could be detected by radar only at distances of a fraction of a kilometre—in other words, a few thousandths of a second before impact. [4]

There are, however, some uses of radar which would be of great value in astronautics. The use of radar altimeters in the approach to a planet has already been mentioned. We may also expect that before any attempt is made to land on Venus a complete radar survey of that enigmatic and permanently cloud-covered world will be made by a ship orbiting at a height of a few hundred kilometres.

---

[4] Far smaller meteors can be detected over great distances once they enter the Earth's atmosphere, but only because they produce an intense ionization trail.

Equipment available even today would give an accurate map of all land and sea areas, if such divisions exist, and would even enable approximate contours to be drawn.

Chapter X

OPENING FRONTIERS

HAVING devoted nine chapters to the "how" of interplanetary flight, it seems only reasonable to spend the last considering the "whither"—and the "why"—of astronautics. Before we expend millions of man-years and, perhaps, an appreciable fraction of the Earth's store of fissile material on the conquest of space, we should certainly have a preliminary glance at the planets to see if it is worth the rather considerable trouble of reaching them. The next few pages, however, must be regarded as the briefest possible introduction to a very large subject, and for further information the reader is referred to the books listed in the Bibliography.

The Moon

There is very little doubt that the Moon, by far the nearest of all astronomical bodies, will be the first to be reconnoitred, the first alien world on which human feet will ever tread. It is the only body whose surface features we have been able to examine closely: in the most powerful telescopes it can be brought to an apparent distance of a few hundred miles and such a wealth of detail is visible that men have spent their entire lives in efforts to record and chart it.

The most characteristic of all the lunar features are the countless "craters", ranging in size from mountain-walled rings 150 miles across to pits a fraction of a mile in diameter. Whether they are due to internal volcanic causes or to meteoric bombardment ages ago is still unsettled, and probably both forces played a part in their formation.

A typical lunar landscape is shown in Plate XII, which is a photograph of one of the dark areas—the so-called "Seas" or "Maria" (*Mare Imbrium*). It shows fine examples of the chief lunar formations—the walled plains, the great mountain ranges, and the tiny crater pits, as well as various rills, ridges and isolated peaks. This region is one of the flattest on the Moon, and other parts are far more mountainous.

The total area of the Moon equals a fifth of the Earth's land surface, but only half of it has been mapped owing to the annoying circumstance that one face is always turned away from us. This is owing to tidal-braking in the remote past, which has stopped the Moon's rotation relative to the Earth. There is, however, not the slightest reason to suppose that the far side is much different from the one we can see.

The Moon is almost completely airless, with, it seems, just sufficient atmosphere to stop meteors and, perhaps, to provide an ionized layer which may be useful for radio communication around its steeply-curving surface. The horizon, because of the Moon's small radius, is only half as far away as on the Earth, and from the centre of the larger craters the surrounding walls would be out of sight.

The absence of atmosphere has a number of very important effects, the most obvious being that it will be impossible for men to work unprotected on the lunar surface.

Outside the airtight and possibly underground settlements which will have to be built, it will always be necessary to wear spacesuits. The exploration of the Moon will therefore be a slow and difficult business, perhaps largely conducted in pressurized caterpillar vehicles which will be capable of negotiating all but the worst terrain. The fact that the Moon's gravity is only a sixth of the Earth's will be a great help both to men and machines (see Plate XII).

There is no twilight on the Moon, no soft transition between night and day, as is shown by the knife-edge shadows on Plate XII. The temperature extremes are therefore equally violent: at noon, in latitudes where the Sun is vertically overhead, the exposed rocks may reach the temperature of boiling water. Towards evening, as the Sun descends through the seven-day-long lunar afternoon, the temperature falls to freezing and far below. Even when the Sun is still above the horizon, its slanting rays can barely warm the powdered pumice and meteoric dust that lies thickly across the Moon's surface; and with the coming of the long night the temperature falls to 150° C. below zero (−240°F.). These extremes, however, only occur at the exposed surface. A few feet underground, or in caves, the temperature would be almost constant day and night.

Free water cannot exist on the Moon, except perhaps as hoar-frost in the early morning or during the 14 days of lunar night. Nevertheless the names of the "Seas", given to the darker areas by imaginative astonomers before the invention of the telescope, have been retained. Some of the lunar names are very beautiful, however inappropriate: "Sea of Serenity", "Marsh of Sleep", "Bay of Rainbows".

The almost complete absence of air and water, and the

fierce temperature extremes, would seem to render any form of natural life on the Moon impossible. There is, however, considerable though not yet conclusive evidence that some form of vegetation may spring up during the lunar day in certain regions, becoming dormant again during the night[1]. Curious dark areas which seem to change their position and appearance have been detected near certain craters (e.g. Aristarchus) and their behaviour is very suggestive of vegetation.

As far as can be foreseen at present, the great importance of the Moon will be as an astronomical observatory and as a stepping-stone to the planets. The problem of setting up a self-supporting lunar colony or outpost is technically a fascinating one, on which speculation is perhaps premature until we know more about our satellite's resources. But it seems reasonable to suppose that all the elements existing on the Earth are also present on the Moon, even if in different combinations, and given power they can be released and used to provide water, air, and materials for closed-cycle systems of horticulture.

Mars and Venus

It is debatable whether Mars or Venus will be the first of the planets to be reached. As we have seen, the journey to Mars is considerably easier, though longer, than that to Venus, but they will both become technically feasible at about the same time. It is to Mars, however, that all

---

[1] This possibility has been vividly described by H. G. Wells in *The First Men in the Moon*.

thoughts will turn as soon as the conquest of the Moon has been assured, for on Mars alone have we been able to detect what is almost certainly the evidence of life.

Though Mars is a small world, its land area is almost as great as that of our own planet owing to the absence of seas. It has a very tenuous but rather deep atmosphere, which is usually cloudless though it sometimes shows extensive areas of haze. The planet itself exhibits distinctive and permanent markings, which careful telescopic examination resolves into masses of fine detail at the very limits of visibility. The interpretation of this elusive detail, which is glimpsed only at the rare moments of perfect seeing, has caused the most famous of all astronomical controversies—the battle of the Martian canals.

A good deal of information about Mars is not, however, in dispute. The planet has three main types of marking—the brilliant white polar caps, the reddish-ochre "deserts", which cover most of the planet, and the smaller blue-green "seas" (see Plate XV.)

It is believed that the "deserts" really are deserts, but the seas, like those of the Moon, are not water-covered. They are much more interesting, for they show seasonal changes which most astronomers now believe are due to the existence of vegetation. During the Martian winter they are chocolate-brown, changing to green or blue-green in the spring and summer. As the spring advances over a Martian hemisphere, so the polar cap shrinks, vanishing completely by midsummer. It is almost certainly composed of a thin layer of ice or hoar-frost, and with its disappearance the "seas" become darker as if their vegetation is being quickened by the arrival of the precious moisture. This darkening spreads down from the Pole during the spring, but with the end of summer the "seas" become less conspicuous, the Polar cap renews itself, and the long winter begins again.

Whatever plant life exists on Mars, it must be exceedingly hardy and perhaps unlike any on the Earth. Although at noon in the Martian summer it can become as hot as it ever does in the temperate regions of our world, the Martian night, even on the equator, is colder than our Antarctic. Moreover the main constituent of the extremely tenuous atmosphere appears to be carbon dioxide: no trace of oxygen has yet been detected. No form of animal life of even a remotely terrestrial nature would be likely under such circumstances.

The existence of intelligence on Mars, either in the past or at the present, can remain only a matter of speculation until the planet has been reached—though it might conceivably be settled by telescopic observation under the perfect seeing conditions on the Moon. At the close of the nineteenth century the reported discovery of a network of fine lines or "canals" covering the planet aroused intense interest and the theory was put forward by the great American astronomer Percival Lowell that they were due to waterways, constructed by a technically very advanced race in a battle against the ever-encroaching deserts. The actual waterways (or, perhaps, pipelines) would of course have been invisible, but the belts of vegetation they fertilized could be seen from Earth, just as the Nile Valley and its yearly crops might be observed from another planet.

Some of the larger canals undoubtedly exist and have even been photographed, but most modern astronomers believe that the finer network which Lowell and his school observed is an optical illusion. This point will certainly be decided as soon as it is possible to set up even a small telescope on the Moon, if not before.

Mars possesses two tiny moons, Phobos and Deimos. They are only a few miles in diameter and so would not be very impressive objects in the planet's sky.

If Mars is an enigma, we know even less about Venus, despite the fact that she comes closer to us than any other planet. There are two reasons for this: one is that, at her nearest, she is between us and the Sun and so is quite invisible. Much more serious, however, is the fact that she is entirely covered with a vast blanket of cloud which has never, in all the years that men have been observing her, opened to give a definite view of the surface beneath. As a result we do not even know her period of rotation, but it is believed that the Venusian "day" may be several of our weeks in length.

This lack of knowledge is particularly exasperating as Venus is very nearly the same size as the Earth and might be expected to resemble our planet in many respects— including habitability. The sunlit side is hot, but not excessively so, for the thick atmospheric blanket helps to maintain a uniform temperature between the dark and the light hemispheres. Unfortunately for our hopes of life, all attempts to discover oxygen or water vapour in the Venusian atmosphere have so far failed completely: instead, the spectroscope has revealed the presence of enormous quantities of carbon dioxide. The clouds that hide the planet are not, therefore, of water vapour, and no satisfactory theory exists to account for them. Venus, in fact, is almost literally shrouded in mystery. No doubt there will be several cautious radar surveys of the hidden surface before any attempt is made to reach it: in the rather unlikely event of intelligent life being there, our arrival will certainly be a shock since the perpetual clouds would, presumably have prevented any discovery of the outside universe.

The Outer Giants

Beyond Mars, going outwards from the Sun, the scale of the Solar System increases. Not only are the planets much further apart, but they are far larger than the inner worlds, and they possess not single moons, but ten or more. Jupiter, Saturn, Uranus and Neptune all have features in common which make them seem of an altogether different birth from the "terrestrial" planets Earth, Mars and Venus. They have immensely deep atmospheres of methane and ammonia—so deep, in fact, that in their lower regions the gases must be liquified under pressures we have never attained on Earth. Though they are exceedingly cold, they are by no means frozen into immobility and on both Jupiter and Saturn great disturbances and eruptions occur—some of them larger than our entire world and persisting for many years.

It is difficult to imagine how any physical exploration of these giant planets will ever be possible, but between them they possess at least 27 satellites, some considerably larger than our Moon. (See Plate XIV) One—Titan, sixth moon of Saturn—is so large that it possesses an extensive atmosphere, being the only satellite to do so. The exploration of all these worlds will be a tremendous undertaking which may well occupy mankind for centuries. They are so far away that we know practically nothing about them, except their approximate diameters and masses. From these it appears that there is something very peculiar about several of Saturn's satellites—their densities being less than that of water!

This general ignorance has not prevented astronomers from giving some of these moons very attractive names, of which perhaps Uranus' satellites have the prettiest—Ariel, Umbriel, Oberon, Titania and Miranda. Saturn's moons have all been named from classical mythology but for some reason seven of Jupiter's extensive family have never been christened and are referred to merely by numbers. There are probably many more of these little worlds still to be discovered, but all those of any size have almost certainly been detected.

Mercury and Pluto

It may seem odd to bracket together the innermost and the outermost planets, but apart from their considerable temperature differences (lead would melt on Mercury, while air would be liquid on Pluto) they appear to have several points in common. They belong to the "terrestial" group of planets, not to the family of semi-gaseous giants, and both may resemble the Moon in composition and general airlessness.

Mercury keeps one face always towards the Sun and consequently has no days or nights as we know them. One hemisphere is perpetually roasted whereas the night side may well be the coldest place in the Solar System—colder even than Pluto. Near the dividing line, however, the temperature would be moderate and would not handicap exploration.

Very little is known about Pluto, which was only discovered in 1930, and even its mass and diameter are uncertain. It is believed to be about the size of the Earth and may be the first of a new series of outer planets, for it appears considerably lighter than theory would lead one to expect. Neither Mercury nor Pluto (as far as is known) possess any satellites.

*   *   *   *

This very cursory survey has by no means exhausted the Solar System—even if we decide, for our purposes, to ignore that somewhat important body, the Sun. Scattered across the planetary orbits, though mostly lying between Mars and Jupiter, are the paths of literally thousands of asteroids or minor planets, the largest of which is about 800 kilometres (500 miles) in diameter. In addition, an unknown number of comets wanders in and out of the system on orbits of varying eccentricity, some taking a few years to go round the Sun, others requiring hundreds of centuries. Although mostly gas, some comets appear to possess solid nuclei which undergo strange transformations as the Sun is approached: but the laws which govern their behaviour (and, even, in some cases, their orbits) are largely unknown.

The most important information, from the point of view of astronautics, about the planets and larger satellites has been assembled for convenience of reference in Table 6.

This, then, is the Solar System; and at first sight it may not appear a very attractive place, although it is certainly an interesting one with plenty of variety. The planets, as far as we know today, are all too hot or too cold, or have other disadvantages of a still more fundamental nature, to make them habitable by human beings. Certainly there can be no question of colonizing them in the relatively

Table 6

Body	Distance from Sun (10⁶ kms.)	Radius —(kms.)	Surface Area (Earth=1)	Gravity (Earth=1)	Day	Escape velocity (km./Sec.)	Atmosphere
Mercury	58	2,400	0.14	0.26	88d	3.5	None
Venus	108	6,100	0.91	0.90	?	10	CO_2+?
Earth	150	6,370	1	1	24h	11.2	N_2+O_2
Moon		1,740	0.07	0.16	27d	2.3	None
Mars	228	3,400	0.28	0.38	25h	5.0	CO_2+?
Phobos		10					None
Deimos		5					None
Jupiter	779	70,000	120	2.65	10h	60	CH_4+NH_3
Io		1,700	0.07	0.1	?	2.3	None
Europa		1,500	0.06	0.1	?	2.0	None
Ganymede		2,600	0.17	0.2	?	2.9	None
Callisto		2,500	0.15	0.2	?	2.2	None
+7 others							
Saturn	1,430	60,000	84	1.14	10h	35	CH_4
Titan		2,800	0.2	0.2	?	3.0	CH_4
Rhea		900				0.7	None
+7 others							None
Uranus	2,870	25,000	15	1	11h	22	CH_4
+5 moons							
Neptune	4,500	26,000	17	1	16h	23	CH_4
Triton		2,500	0.15	0.2	?	3.0	None?
+1 other							
Pluto	5,900	?	?	?	?	?	?

easy way that the unknown lands of our own world were opened up in the past. Against this, we must not forget that we now possess far greater technical powers to match the challenge of hostile environments. Professor Fritz Zwicky, one of the world's leading astrophysicists, has suggested that eventually the use of atomic engineering will enable us to shape the other planets to suit our needs—and even, if necessary, to alter their orbits.

It is more than probable, however, that the most important material uses of the planets will be in directions totally unexpected today. This has often been the case in the history of exploration on our own Earth. In his vain search for gold, Columbus certainly never dreamed of the far greater treasure that would one day gush from the oil-wells of the New World; and the first men to survey the barren wastes of the Canadian Arctic—which to many must have seemed as unrewarding as the deserts of the Moon—could never have guessed of the faintly-radio-active metal that lay guarding its secrets beneath their feet.

No one can ever foresee what role a new land may play in history; and we are considering now not merely new countries, or even continents—but worlds.

No investment pays better dividends to humanity than scientific research, though it sometimes has to wait a century or two for the profits. Some of the scientific repercussions of space flight have already been mentioned, and could be multiplied indefinitely. It is not merely the physical sciences which will benefit: consider, for example, the possibilities of medical research opened up by "free-fall" or low-gravity conditions. Who can say how much our lives are shortened by the heart's continual battle against gravity? On the Moon, sufferers from cardiac trouble might live normal lives—and normal lives might be greatly prolonged. This is only a random example of the way astronautics might conceivably affect mankind vitally and directly.

But the important consequences of space flight, and the main reasons for its accomplishment, are intangible, and to understand them we must look not to the future but to the past. Although man has occupied the greater part of the habitable globe for thousands of years, until only five centuries ago he lived—psychologically—not in one world but in many. Each of the great cultures in the belt from Britain to Japan was insulated from its neighbours by geography or deliberate choice: each was convinced that it alone represented the flower of civilization, and that all else was barbarism.

The "Unification of the world", to use Toynbee's somewhat optimistic phrase, became possible only when the sailing ship and the arts of navigation were developed sufficiently to replace the difficult overland routes by the easier sea-passages. The result was the great age of exploration whose physical climax was the discovery of the Americas, and whose supreme intellectual achievement was the liberation of the human spirit. Perhaps no better symbol of the questing mind of Renaissance man could be found than the lonely ship sailing steadfastly towards new horizons, until east and west had merged at last and the circumnavigation of the globe had been achieved.

First by land, then by sea, man grew to know his planet; but its final conquest was to lie in a third element, and by means beyond the imagination of almost all men who had ever lived before the twentieth century. The swiftness with which mankind has lifted its commerce and its wars into the air has surpassed the wildest fantasy. Now indeed we have fulfilled the poet's dream and can "ride secure the cruel sky". Through this mastery the last unknown lands have been opened up: over the road along which Alexander burnt out his life, the businessmen and civil servants now pass in comfort in a matter of hours.

The victory has been complete, yet in the winning it has turned to ashes. Every age but ours has had its El Dorado, its Happy Isles, or its North-West Passage to lure the adventurous into the unknown. A lifetime ago men could still dream of what might lie at the poles—but soon the North Pole will be the cross-roads of the world. We may try to console ourselves with the thought that even if Earth has no new horizons, there are no bounds to the endless frontier of science. Yet it may be doubted if this is enough, for only very sophisticated minds are satisfied with purely intellectual adventures.

The importance of exploration does not lie merely in the opportunities it gives to the adolescent (but not to be despised) desires for excitement and variety. It is no mere accident that the age of Columbus was also the age of Leonardo, or that Sir Walter Raleigh was a contemporary of Shakespeare and Galileo. "In human records", wrote the anthropologist J. D. Unwin, "there is no trace of any display of productive energy which has not been preceded by a display of expansive energy". And today, all possibility of expansion on Earth itself has practically ceased.

The thought is a sombre one. Even if it survives the hazards of war, our culture is proceding under a momentum which must be exhausted in the foreseeable future. Fabre once described how he linked the two ends of a chain of marching caterpillars so that they circled endlessly in a closed loop. Even if we avoid all other disasters, this would appear a fitting symbol of humanity's eventual fate when the impetus of the last few centuries has reached its peak and died away. For a closed culture, though it may endure for centuries, is inherently unstable. It may decay quietly and crumble into ruin, or it may be disrupted violently by internal conflicts. Space travel is a necessary, though not in itself a sufficient, way of escape from this predicament.

It is now four hundred years since Copernicus destroyed mediæval cosmology and dethroned the Earth from the centre of creation. Shattering though the repercussions of that fall were in the fields of science and philosophy, they scarcely touched the ordinary man. To him this planet is still the whole of the universe: he knows that other worlds exist, but the knowledge does not affect his life and therefore has little real meaning to him.

All this will be changed before the twentieth century draws to its end. Into a few decades may be compressed more profound alterations in our world picture than occurred during the whole of the Renaissance and the age of discovery that followed. To our grandchildren the Moon may become what the Americas were four hundred years ago—a world of unknown danger, promise and opportunity. No longer will Mars and Venus be merely the names of wandering lights seldom glimpsed by the dwellers in cities. They will be more familar than ever they were to those eastern watchers who first marked their movements, for they will be the new frontiers of the human mind.

Those new frontiers are urgently needed. The crossing of space—even the mere belief in its possibility—may do much to reduce the tensions of our age by turning men's minds outwards and away from their tribal conflicts. It may well be that only by acquiring this new sense of boundless frontiers will the world break free from the ancient cycle of war and peace. One wonders how even the most stubborn of nationalisms will survive when men have seen the Earth as a pale crescent dwindling against the stars, until at last they look for it in vain.

No doubt there are many who, while agreeing that these things are possible, will shrink from them in horror, hoping that they will never come to pass. They remember Pascal's terror of the silent spaces between the stars, and are overwhelmed by the nightmare immensities which Victorian astronomers were so fond of evoking. Such an outlook is somewhat naive, for the meaningless millions of miles between the Sun and its outermost planets are no more, and no less, impressive than the vertiginous gulf lying between the electron and the atomic nucleus. Mere distance is nothing: only the time that is needed to span it has any meaning. A spaceship which can reach the Moon at all would require less time for the journey than a stage-coach once took to travel the length of England. When the atomic drive is reasonably efficient, the nearer planets would be only a few weeks from Earth, and so will seem scarcely more remote than are the antipodes today.

It is fascinating, however premature, to try and imagine the pattern of events when the Solar System is opened up to mankind. In the footsteps of the first explorers will follow the scientists and engineers, shaping strange environments with technologies as yet unborn. Later will come the colonists, laying the foundations of cultures which in time may surpass those of the mother world. The torch of civilisation has dropped from failing fingers too often before for us to imagine that it will never be handed on again.

We must not let our pride in our achievements blind us to the lessons of history. Over the first cities of mankind, the desert sands now lie centuries deep. Could the builders of Ur and Babylon—once the wonders of the world—have pictured London or New York? Nor can we imagine the citadels that our descendants may build beneath the blinding sun of Mercury, or under the stars of the cold Plutonian wastes. And beyond the planets, though ages still ahead of us in time, lies the unknown and infinite promise of the stars.

There will, it is true, be danger in space, as there has always been on the oceans or in the air. Some of these dangers we may guess: others we shall not know until we meet them. Nature is no friend of man's, and the most that he can hope for is her neutrality. But if he meets destruction, it will be at his own hands and according to a familiar pattern.

The dream of flight was one of the noblest, and one of the most disinterested, of all man's aspirations. Yet it led in the end to that silver Superfortress driving in passionless beauty through August skies towards the city whose name it was to sear into the conscience of the world. Already there has been half-serious talk in the United States concerning the use of the Moon for military bases and launching sites. The crossing of space may thus bring, not a new Renaissance, but the final catastrophe which haunts our generation.

That is the danger, the dark thundercloud that threatens the promise of the dawn. The rocket has already been the instrument of evil, and may be so again. But there is no way back into the past: the choice, as Wells once said, is the Universe—or nothing. Though men and civilisations may yearn for rest, for the Elysian dream of the Lotos Eaters, that is a desire that merges imperceptibly into death. The challenge of the great spaces between the worlds is a stupendous one; but if we fail to meet it, the story of our race will be drawing to its close. Humanity will have turned its back upon the still untrodden heights and will be descending again the long slope that stretches, across a thousand million years of time, down to the shores of the primeval sea.

MATHEMATICAL APPENDIX

Chapter II

If g is the value of gravity at the Earth's surface, and R = Earth's radius, then at a radial distance r, gravity is given by Newton's inverse square law as

$$g_r = g\frac{R^2}{r^2} \qquad \dots \qquad \dots \qquad (II.1)$$

Thus the work E in moving unit mass from R to infinity is given by

$$E = \int_R^\infty g\frac{R^2}{r^2}\, dr = gR \qquad \dots \qquad (II.2)$$

Similarly the work in moving unit mass from an external point r to infinity is

$$E_r = \int_r^\infty g\frac{R^2}{r^2}\, dr = \frac{gR^2}{r} \qquad \dots \qquad (II.3)$$

To project a body from the Earth's surface to infinity it must, by Equation II.2, be given a kinetic energy of gR per unit mass. Hence the escape velocity V is given by

$$\tfrac{1}{2}V^2 = gR$$

$$\text{or } V = \sqrt{2gR} \qquad \dots \qquad \dots \qquad (II.4)$$

Similarly, from Equation II.3, the escape velocity V_r at a distance r is given by

$$\tfrac{1}{2}V_r^2 = \frac{gR^2}{r}$$

$$\text{or } V_r = \sqrt{\frac{2gR^2}{r}} \qquad \dots \qquad (II.5)$$

Hence V_r varies inversely as the square *root* of the distance from the Earth's centre.

The distance from the Earth attained by projection at less than escape velocity can be readily calculated by energy considerations. If the body comes to rest at a radial distance r, then the work done against gravity equals the initial kinetic energy, or

$$\int_R^r g\frac{R^2}{r^2}\ dr = \tfrac{1}{2}V^2$$

$$\therefore\ V^2 = 2gR^2\left[\frac{1}{R} - \frac{1}{r}\right]\quad\ldots\quad(II.6)$$

$$\text{Hence } r = \frac{2gR^2}{2gR - V^2}\quad\ldots\quad(II.7)$$

or the altitude from the Earth's surface is given by

$$h = \frac{2gR^2}{2gR - V^2} - R\ \ldots\ (II.7a)$$

which becomes infinite when $V^2 = 2gR$, as in Equation II.4.

For a body to be maintained in a circular orbit radius r, the outward centrifugal force must equal the inwards gravitational attraction, and hence

$$\frac{V_r^2}{r} = \frac{gR^2}{r^2}$$

$$\text{Hence } V_r = \sqrt{\frac{gR^2}{r}}\quad\ldots\quad(II.8)$$

Near the Earth's surface this becomes

$$V = \sqrt{gR}\quad\ldots\quad(II.8a)$$

Comparison with Equations II.4 and II.5 shows that at any point the escape velocity is $\sqrt{2}$ times the circular velocity at that point.

The time of revolution in a circular orbit radius r is given immediately from II.8, being equal to

$$\frac{2\pi r}{V_r} = \sqrt{\frac{2\pi r^{\frac{3}{2}}}{gR^2}} \quad \ldots \quad (II.9)$$

which is Kepler's Third Law of planetary motion for the special case of a circular orbit.

* * * *

The equations of motion in conic section orbits will not be derived here, as they may be found in any dynamics text-book. (e.g. Lamb's or Ramsay's "Dynamics"). Only the more important results will be collected for convenience of reference.

If the centre of force is at S, the velocity V at any point

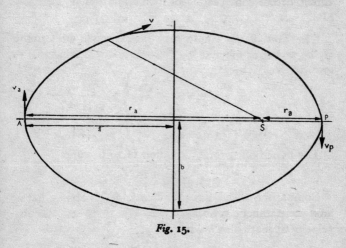

Fig. 15.

distance r from S is given, for an elliptic orbit, by:—

$$V^2 = \mu \left(\frac{2}{r} - \frac{1}{a} \right) \quad \dots \quad \dots \quad (II.10)$$

where μ is a constant for any gravitational field, equal to gR^2, and a is the semi-major axis.

At A (see Figure 15), where $r_a = a(1+e)$, e being the eccentricity, this equation becomes

$$V_a^2 = \frac{\mu}{a} \cdot \frac{1-e}{1+e} \quad \dots \quad \dots \quad (II.11)$$

At P, where $r_p = a(1-e)$

$$V_p^2 = \frac{\mu}{a} \cdot \frac{1+e}{1-e} \quad \dots \quad \dots \quad (II.12)$$

Hence $\dfrac{V_p}{V_a} = \dfrac{1+e}{1-e} \quad \dots \quad (II.13)$

Hence also the important result (which may be obtained directly from conservation of momentum) that

$$V_p r_p = V_a r_a \quad \dots \quad (II.14)$$

The axes of the ellipse may be expressed in terms of μ, V_p and r_p as follows:

$$\left.\begin{aligned} a &= \frac{\mu}{(2\mu/r_p) - V_p^2} \\[2mm] b &= \sqrt{\frac{V_p r_p}{(2\mu/r_p) - V_p^2}} \end{aligned}\right\} \quad \dots \ (II.15)$$

For hyperbolic orbits, Equation II.10 becomes

$$V^2 = \mu \left(\frac{2}{r} + \frac{1}{a} \right)$$

and for parabolic orbits

$$V^2 = 2\mu/r$$

Chapter III

If the instantaneous mass of the rocket is m, its exhaust velocity c, and the rate of mass-flow dm/dt, then the thrust developed is c.dm/dt. Hence the equation of motion is:

$$\frac{m\,dV}{dt} = -c\,\frac{dm}{dt} \quad \dots \quad (III.1)$$

which on integration over the time of burning gives

$$V = c\,\log_e\frac{M_o}{M_t} = c\,\log_e R \quad \dots \quad (III.2)$$

*   *   *   *

Let the rocket propellants, after combustion, attain a temperature $T°$ absolute and a pressure p_1. T is determined by the nature of the propellants—their available chemical energy, the mixture ratio at which they are used, and the specific heat of their gaseous products. It is affected only slightly by p_1, through the mechanism of the reverse dissociation reactions.

The nozzle now accepts the gases flowing into it from the combustion chamber and expands them down to a lower exit pressure p_2, thereby converting their internal pressure and temperature energy as fully as possible into kinetic energy of the emergent jet. The application of the classic Bernoulli relation for adiabatic flow of a compressible fluid shows that for an ideal gas of molecular weight M, expansion under these circumstances gives an exhaust velocity c according to this equation:—

$$c = \sqrt{\frac{2\gamma}{\gamma-1}\cdot\frac{GT}{M}\left\{1-\left(\frac{p_2}{p_1}\right)^{\frac{\gamma-1}{\gamma}}\right\}} \quad \dots \quad \dots \quad (III.3)$$

where G is the universal gas constant and γ the ratio of the specific heats of the gas.

For any given gas mixture, γ is a constant (and does not vary much for most of the different mixtures of practical interest); the expansion ratio p_2/p_1, is also fixed for a motor operating under given conditions. Hence we can write the approximate relation:—

$$c \simeq k \sqrt{\dfrac{T}{M}} \qquad \dots \qquad (III.4)$$

where k is a constant for the particular case under consideration, and will in fact not vary greatly for any type of rocket motor. For motors operating in vacuum, $k=0.25$ will give c correct to about ± 10 per cent. in most practical cases, when the units are km/sec and degrees K.

Chapter IV

If the acceleration (assumed constant) of the rocket is ng, the time t to reach the final velocity V is V/ng. But, if air resistance is neglected,

$$V = c \log_e R - gt$$

$$= c \log_e R - \dfrac{V.}{n}$$

$$\therefore V \dfrac{n+1}{n} = c \log_e R$$

Hence the mass-ratio R_n required at any acceleration ng is

$$R_n = e^{\dfrac{V}{c}\dfrac{n+1}{n}} \qquad \dots \qquad \dots \qquad (IV.2)$$

Chapter V

The duration of a journey from the neighbourhood of the Earth to that of the Moon (neglecting the effect of the Moon's field) may be calculated as follows for the three cases of rectilinear motion that arise.

(1) INITIAL VELOCITY JUST SUFFICIENT TO REACH THE MOON (Elliptic Case).

Since the velocity at the Moon's distance (S) is zero, the velocity at any intermediate point r is given, by Equation II.6, by

$$v^2 = 2gR^2\left[\frac{1}{r} - \frac{1}{S}\right] = k^2\left[\frac{1}{r} - \frac{1}{S}\right] \quad \text{say}$$

Hence $v = \dfrac{dr}{dt} = k\left[\dfrac{1}{r} - \dfrac{1}{S}\right]^{\frac{1}{2}}$

This may be readily solved by the substitution $r = S\cos^2\theta$ which gives, after some reduction,

$$kt = -2S^{\frac{3}{2}}\int_{\theta_0}^{\theta}\cos^2\theta\,d\theta$$

Substituting the limits, we obtain

$$t = \frac{S^{\frac{3}{2}}}{k}\left[\theta_0 + \cos\theta_0\sin\theta_0\right] \quad \dots \quad \text{(V.1)}$$

where $\cos^2\theta_0 = R/S$

(2) BODY PROJECTED AT PARABOLIC VELOCITY.

In this case, since $v = 0$ when $r = \infty$, the equation of motion reduces to

$$\frac{dr}{dt} = k\left(\frac{1}{r}\right)^{\frac{1}{2}}$$

whence $t = \dfrac{2}{3k}\left[S^{\frac{3}{2}} - R^{\frac{3}{2}}\right] \quad \dots \quad \dots \quad \text{(V.2)}$

At the distance of the Moon, S is so much larger than R that this can be written

$$t = \frac{2}{3k} S^{\frac{3}{2}}$$

(3) BODY PROJECTED AT MORE THAN ESCAPE VELOCITY
(Hyperbolic Case).

If the initial velocity is v_0 ($> \sqrt{2gR}$) then at any point r the velocity v is given, from energy considerations, by the equation

$$\tfrac{1}{2} v_0^2 - gR = \tfrac{1}{2} v^2 - \frac{gR^2}{r}$$

or $v^2 = v_0^2 - 2gR + \dfrac{2gR^2}{r}$

This may be simplified by introducing the constant S_1, defined by $v_0^2 - 2gR = \dfrac{2gR^2}{S_1}$, whence

$$v^2 = \left(\frac{dr}{dt}\right)^2 = k^2 \left[\frac{1}{r} + \frac{1}{S_1}\right]$$

This equation may be solved by the substitution $r = S_1 \sinh^2\theta$ which gives, after reduction,

$$kt = 2 S_1^{\frac{3}{2}} \int_{\theta_0}^{\theta} \sinh^2\theta \, d\theta$$

Hence $t = \dfrac{S_1^{\frac{3}{2}}}{k} \left[\theta_0 - \cosh\theta_0 \sinh\theta_0 - \theta + \cosh\theta\sinh\theta\right]$ ...(V.3)

where $\sinh^2\theta_0 = R/S_1$ and $\sinh^2\theta = S/S_1$

For large values of v_0 this can be shown to reduce to

$$t = \frac{S}{\sqrt{v_0^2 - 2gR}} \qquad \ldots \qquad (V.4)$$

a result which is immediately obvious, since the denominator is simply the "velocity at infinity" which the body approaches asymptotically. This equation gives results no more than 5 per cent. too large for velocities of projection over 20 km/sec. At higher velocities it will be still more accurate.

All the above equations may, of course, be used for vertical ascent in any gravitational field if the constants are suitably adjusted. They may thus be used to find the time of radial travel between one planetary orbit and another.

Chapter VII

Consider a rocket mass M, exhaust velocity c, rate of fuel consumption per second m, acceleration ng.

$$\text{Then thrust} = Mng = mc$$

Now the rate at which kinetic energy is being put into the jet must be

$$P = \tfrac{1}{2}mc^2$$
$$\text{Hence } P = \tfrac{1}{2}Mngc \quad \ldots \quad (VII.1)$$

or the "specific exhaust power" per unit mass of ship is

$$p = \tfrac{1}{2}ngc \quad \ldots \quad \ldots \quad (VII.2)$$

If c is in km/sec., p = 4900 nc kilowatts/tonne or 6600 nc H.P./ton.

Chapter IX

TEMPERATURE OF A BODY IN SPACE

Consider a sphere in space: let its radius be r, and the amount of heat intersected per second per cm^2 of area perpendicular to the Sun be s. Assume that it is perfectly absorbing and that its temperature T is uniform over the whole surface. (This condition would be nearly fulfilled for a black-painted body which was slowly rotating or had good conductivity).

Then the energy exchange relation for thermal equilibrium is

$$\pi r^2 s = 4\pi r^2 \sigma T^4 \quad (\sigma = \text{Stefan's constant})$$

$$\text{Hence } T = \left[\frac{s}{4\sigma}\right]^{\frac{1}{4}} \quad \ldots \quad \text{(IX.1)}$$

Now $\sigma = 5.67 \times 10^{-5}$ erg.cm.$^{-2}$ sec.$^{-1}$ deg.$^{-4}$ and at the Earth's distance from the Sun $s = 1.35 \times 10^6$ c.g.s. units. Hence $T = 277°K = 4°C.$ (39°F.).

If the body did not radiate appreciably from the "night side" (e.g. if that was silvered and only the sunward side blackened) then

$$T = \left[\frac{s}{2\sigma}\right]^{\frac{1}{4}} \quad \ldots \quad \ldots \quad \text{(IX.2)}$$

This gives values of 329°K (132°F.) for a body at the Earth's orbit. Intermediate temperatures could be obtained by suitable coating material. It must not be forgotten, moreover, that a considerable amount of heat would be generated by the crew's bodies and the ship's auxiliary mechanisms, so that—at any rate in the neighbourhood of the Earth—the problem is that of discarding excess heat rather than the reverse.

Temperatures elsewhere in the Solar System may be easily obtained from these equations by adjusting the value of s according to the inverse square law. They range from 445°K at Mercury to 44°K at Pluto. (340°F and —380°F, respectively). These figures, of course, bear little relation to the actual surface temperatures of the planets, which are greatly affected by rotation, atmosphere, etc.

*　　　*　　　*　　　*

RADIO RANGES IN SPACE

Let the transmitted power be P_t watts, the received power be P_r watts, the areas of the transmitter and receiver arrays be A_t and A_r square metres, the range be d metres, the wavelength be λ metres. Let the gain of the transmitting array (i.e. the number of times it multiplies the power received at any point over that produced by an omni-directional source) be G_t.

Then by the inverse square law the power density at the receiver is.

$$\frac{G_t P_t}{4\pi d^2}\text{watts/metre}^2$$

Therefore the received power is given by

$$P_r = \frac{G_t P_t A_r}{4\pi d^2}\text{ watts}$$

It can be shown that the gain of a circular array is given approximately by $G = 4\pi A/\lambda^2$. Substituting for G_t thus gives:—

$$P_r = \frac{A_t A_r P_t}{d^2 \lambda^2}$$

$$\text{or } P_t = \frac{d^2 \lambda^2}{A_t A_r}P_r \qquad \cdots \qquad \text{(IX.3)}$$

It may be assumed that the effective areas of the transmitting and receiving arrays are approximately equal to their physical areas. Given the minimum acceptable receiver power P_r required for any type of service, Equation IX.3 thus enables one to estimate the power needed by the transmitter at a given distance.

BIBLIOGRAPHY

This is intended merely as a representative, not exhaustive, list of books on the subject. A practically full bibliography (up to 1947) will be found in the first work listed below.

Astronautics

ROCKETS AND SPACE TRAVEL: Willy Ley. (Viking Press, N.Y.; Chapman & Hall, London.)

An excellent semi-technical account, giving a detailed history of the subject.

THE CONQUEST OF SPACE: Chesley Bonestell and Willy Ley. (Viking Press, N.Y.)

Semi-technical, with magnificent colour plates showing conditions on the planets, according to the best astronomical knowledge.

WEGE ZUR RAUMSCHIFFAHRT: Hermann Oberth. (Oldenbourg, Munich: Edwards Bros., Ann Arbor, U.S.A.).

Highly technical: the classic work which stimulated European interest in space flight.

Rockets

ROCKETS: Robert H. Goddard. (American Rocket Society.)
A reprint of Goddard's original Smithsonian papers.

BALLISTICS OF THE FUTURE: J. M. J. Kooy and J. W. H. Uytenbogaart. (H. Stam, Haarlem.)
    Highly mathematical, but with a detailed description of V.2 with many drawings, etc.

ROCKET PROPULSION ELEMENTS: G. P. Sutton. (Wiley, N.Y.)
    Technical: an excellent text-book for engineers.

THE COMING AGE OF ROCKET POWER: G. E. Pendray. (Harper, N.Y.)
    Semi-technical.

GUIDED MISSILES: A. R. Weyl. (Temple Press).

Astronomy
EARTH, MOON AND PLANETS: F. L. Whipple. (J. & A. Churchill, London: Blakiston, Pa.)

LIFE ON OTHER WORLDS: Sir H. Spencer Jones. (English Universities Press.)

Periodicals
JOURNAL OF THE BRITISH INTERPLANETARY SOCIETY. (Concerned with all aspects of interplanetary flight and related subjects. Papers range from the purely mathematical to literary and philosophical. Published bi-monthly at 157, Friary Rd., London, S.E.15).

JOURNAL OF THE AMERICAN ROCKET SOCIETY. (Concerned chiefly with rocket engineering but papers on astronautics are becoming more frequent. Published quarterly at 29 West 39th St., New York 18).

INDEX

150